TEL AVIV stories

Life, Death, & Love
in Israel's Unholy City

D0595616

ASHLEY RINDSBERG

Copyright © 2010 by Ashley Rindsberg

All rights reserved. No part of this book may be copied or reproduced in any form without the express written consent of the publisher, except for reviewers, who may copy limited passages for the purposes of review.

Author's note:
This is a work of fiction. Any resemblance to actual events, names or persons is purely coincidental.

Cover Image:
Florent Fourniau

First Edition
Midnight Oil Publishing
www.midnightoilpublishing.com

Contents

www.midnightoilpublishing.com

Tel Aviv, Tel Aviv, Tel Aviv!
Like a child that knows enough to mock you
But not to praise you.

Prologue

There are many people in Tel Aviv. Close to a million souls walk its streets, go to the theater, linger in cafes in the sun, make love in quiet rooms, argue on the street, and one day, one way or another, leave. They are too varied for description, these people, and there are too many of them to meaningfully consider. But they, no doubt, are real — each with lives, with histories, with hopes, and beyond the neutrality of this page, with qualities good and bad, beautiful and ugly, saintly, evil and, of course, just plain.

Sitting on a hill, however, as I am, the reality of these lives looks different. From here their figures are blurred beyond recognition: they make no decisions, don't have preferences, and even lack intention. They look more like the shadows of the dead — damned not to live. They come, and they go.

But there's another group of people in Tel Aviv. They are the opposite of the first group, and their numbers are much smaller. Up close, you see them and you see nothing — just vacant stares, confused looks, crazy outfits, incomprehensible movements and gestures. They wander around the city seemingly without purpose. They are as likely to turn up in the dirty maze of Hamasger District as on the ivory boulevards around Rothschild. They sometimes peer out from hiding in the hair of ficus trees and sometimes they walk up to you and speak. But all of them are here permanently, forever, and they cannot cease to exist. From here on my lonely hill I can see each of them, and while my interpretation of their actions and words (I can even hear them if I sit still) might be wrong, and as far from the truth as they are from reality, I see them perfectly, clearly, and am assured of their lives.

It may be that they all come from and go to the same place, where they know each other, shake hands, and mingle. It's possible, but I have no evidence to think so — unless, of course, that place is the city itself, Tel Aviv.

Even if it's not their intention, it is the case. And for those who have not been able to see the city built on dunes, even after spending time there, it can be seen and almost completely understood through this human flora. I've given them names and places, and sometimes words, it's true. But then it's even more true that they've given me a name, have provided my place, and donate to me my words.

Here they are: they carry the city in on a tray, serving it to the rest of us who can't understand what it really is, being only shadows ourselves. If you want existence and truth, keep your eyes open. Save your courage (don't waste it in the bars or in making brave statements to professors) and speak to them. I have crawled up to this hill after years of crawling. I'm tired and frustrated but turning to look back down I realize I can finally see. I realize I can see, but as I watch these twisted figures of humanity go about their rituals I also realize that my life is down there, that I am among them but separate from them, like them but different, able to hear them but utterly unable to speak.

Spinoza Street

I turned right onto Spinoza Street since it was cool outside for the first time in eight months and I thought that the leaf-lined streets and hidden apartment buildings would be a better way home than the choked sidewalks of Saturday streets in the city. The street was empty and quiet. Cats, as usual, walked their beats, occasionally scrowling and hissing when an intruding animal crossed an invisible line of territory. Above, in their chaotic unison, bats flapped around, climbing up and then falling down to swoop past a low-hanging branch and snatch a drooping fruit. The moon gave some light but kept its distance. The whole place was moist and fresh as if the city were a humid garden with all its strange buildings growing like exotic trees and flowers, and the human insects walking back and forth on the twigs and leaves.

Spinoza Street was just another vein on one of the many million leaves. Thirty steps down the street and I was set back deep within myself, trying to remember the lyrics to a song; doing calculations of my income and outcome; thinking of some things I'd said to a woman a few days before. In short: contemplating my life.

I was passing an old, toothless Bauhaus building when I heard someone mumble a few words. I turned my head toward the sound but kept walking. The voice repeated the string of sounds. I looked again and saw a man edge forward from the shadows of a ficus tree. He stood in front of a large plastic garbage bin on wheels that was filled with filthy but neatly stacked cardboard boxes, discarded pillows, blankets, and other things. From the sides of the bin hung heavy bags that sorted glass bottles, metal pieces, small electronics, and various chunks of plastic.

The man himself wore heavy pants beneath shorts. He had on a few sweaters and one or two jackets. Around his neck was wrapped the scarf of a desert wanderer. All his clothes and garments were dinged by the street but arranged on his body with care, with consciousness, it seemed, of his image.

His face was the most amazing and most

cunning part of this getup. His thick gray hair with streaks of white and yellow swirled to the side and then swooped down his neck almost gallantly. His eyes were placid but observant, his face tanned with experience, his mouth silent with thought and wary of ignorance. He wore a trimmed Spanish mustache that came to points on either side. And below it, a thicket of gray and yellow hair swirled into a conical goatee that pointed sharply.

He stood there allowing the moon to put light on him. He wore a backpack and had one hand on his hip. "For dell, for all dell on."

"What?" I asked.

"Can you spare a few shekels?" he said in perfect English, with a rich but indecipherable accent.

"I'm sorry," I responded, not quite answering the question.

"Why be sorry? Did you not pervade the thing with volition? Were you not to give without giving? The sorry are those who come from the poor."

"I… I don't understand."

"You think I'm poor?"

"No, I—"

"Am only thought poor. But in fact am not poor. Not rich. Not poor. I got what I want and don't want what I need. Can you spare a few shekels?"

I couldn't understand it but hearing the man affirm that he was not poor made me more willing to give him the money that he asked for but, apparently, didn't need. I fished my wallet out of my pocket and got rid of twenty shekels.

I turned to keep walking but stopped myself and without a thought said, "Can I ask you something?"

The man looked at me, grunted and made a nod that was only noticeable by the downward movement of his goatee. "How did you get here?"

"I walked," he said quietly.

"No, I mean how did you get to this... situation?"

He looked at me for a moment, or maybe more than a moment, trying to fathom the motive behind my question. I could see his mind, limber but literal, lapping at his unconscious, putting grains of memory on the shore, taking others back to its depth.

"You fear it, son," he said, looking off to the side.

"Fear what?"

"This."

"Homelessness? Yes, I guess I do. But most do."

"Ah forun. I un. No this isn't homelessness. What is it? It's everything. It's the unfolding. It's the wreck of the world. It's everything.

"Phhhh," the old man said. "You're afraid, you are afraid. Well I'll tell you how I got here, what brought me here, what took me across this little bathtub world of ours, what taught me the seven languages, how I looked at the sky and thought it needs renovating, how I looked at the green hills and all the sand and found them to be nothing. But keep quiet because this story requires concentration.

"I was a young man. Older than you are now but still young. I presume that I looked like I now look. My wife was the great beauty of the countryside. I found her sifting sallies in the fields one day and from then on I followed her around like a lost goat until she came to accept the tow. Eventually I made it to her father's dinner table where the old man and his steel-wool wife treated me like a burnt dish. Only the young ones really liked me since I snickered at them, made loops with my tongue when the adults' eyes were closed for the prayer.

"Malena's mute acceptance of me gradually slid into passionate love. I'd followed her around the countryside for months by that point. At first, she was afraid and she'd run, watching me pursue her from the corner of her eye. Then I became a nuisance and she turned to show me the way or point me toward the city. Finally, I became to her a part of nature — a goat looking at her with earnest goat eyes. After so much of my looking, she looked back. And then she couldn't stop looking.

"The first time I went to their home she didn't bring me there so much as let me in. The family's rough, simple values didn't allow them to refuse something that had a beating heart and didn't show signs of danger. So I sat at their table and in the morning the father would slide open the barn door, where I slept, and hurl a biscuit or two at me and then walk off toward the tractor shed — leaving me with the expectation that I should follow behind him.

"After a few months of this silent routine, the girl snuck into the barn one night after dinner and took off my old goat's skin and found a naked man underneath, living for the woman, breathing for the woman, eating for the woman and even shitting for the woman who stood in front of him. For the space of no more than two seconds as she stared at me, transfiguring me from a four-legged animal into an upright (if downtrodden) man, I experienced the perfect bliss of existing as a satyr. I could feel my shaggy goat legs keeping me warm, I could feel the massive need of strength, the desire to trample, the eternity of each cell in my body.

"Malena moved to kiss me and I flinched for a split second and the flinch, the hesitation of a greedy thought, completed the transformation and I was again a man. She sensed the flinch even if she didn't see it with her eyes or feel it with her hands. It was like she tasted it in her mouth. And that was the beginning of the end of our romance.

"At the dinner table I threw small, polite but exasperating fits that I expressed by almost slamming my cup on the table, scratching the knife against the plate and, to really torture those simple, scornful country people, praying louder than the rest of them during grace.

"I threw my ego around the room and spared no one. Even the young children — still too young to be contemptuous — were targeted. When I knew they were peeping through half-closed eyes or split fingers during prayer, hoping and wishing for their secret prayer-time friend to delight them once in their dreary day, I'd close my eyes tighter, purse my lips together and grumble the prayers for the meal harshly.

"During the day I was crazed with work. I took the reigns of the old man's farming operations. I begged him to modernize. I persuaded him to streamline. I browbeat him into profiting by the clump of dry clay he called a farm.

"It took a year to transform the poor, old roughshod farm into a produce and livestock operation that sold even the chickenshit for a profit. I took a salary that was fair and I never took more or less than that. At the end of two years I went to the old man and informed him I'd be marrying his daughter and that he could send a message to all the bumpkin suitors that they could head home.

"The old man, sitting in a silk robe that my labor had earned him, roasting by a fire burning logs that my ingenuity had cultivated and harvested, straightened up and pretended to take my demand as a request. 'Well, I'll have to speak with the girl's mother about this. And you and I should sit down and talk for a moment.' I sat down, endured two minutes of lecture, and a few weeks later took his daughter.

"The marriage was fine. I loved the girl. In the

mornings of our marriage I'd wake up and try to drown myself in her black eyes and hair, and then she'd wake up and I could relax and rest on the white shores of her arms and breasts.

"The money came in. Our house grew. There were children. We had friends and cars and a city apartment to complement the suburban house. I 'shaved with cream' as my father-in-law began saying after we started to make real money.

"But the girl began to notice things, almost before I did. I'd lost interest in the moneymaking. Our children were fine on their own, gently indifferent to their father's love when they had the abundance of their mother. Malena had grown older but not less beautiful, not less lovely. But my ego was satisfied. The father- and mother-in-law who had once restrained themselves from throwing chicken bones at me now scraped the floor in front of me. My colleagues loved me. My enemies calmly detested me. That tired monster within me wanted its rage back but it had nothing to rage for.

"I looked into the sky of the universe. I started looking into the difficult blackness. Malena saw it in my eyes. She'd look at me like she was trying to peer through a foggy window. But I knew — I knew the truth. I knew, or began to know, to see, the immortality of my inward vision. I started to see things without looking: I could look down and see the geography of morality laid out like a road map. I could see the passing of actions in and out of the barrier between life and living. I began to see the giant tally, the chimera of daily life, the abyss.

"She knew my secret. I knew she knew. What I didn't know (what she didn't know either) was what to do about it.

"It was a risky situation. 'Anything could happen,' I repeated over and over in my mind until I started saying it aloud. I was tortured by the dilemma — by her, by my love and admiration for her, her beauty, her simplicity, her perfection. And I was threatened with the loss of everything — with my life's work which I knew I hadn't truly begun but had almost finished laying the foundation for. A choice had to be made. What would you have — No. There was only one choice, I knew it, and painful choices are not necessarily wrong ones.

"I emerged from myself so I could put things in action. It hurt me so much to see that Malena misunderstood. She thought I was 'coming back' to her, as she said once during dinner. Holding my glass

I simply smiled the devil's smile and swallowed my memories of her and knew that the time had come.

"The men arrived the next morning. The bedroom was quiet and cool from the darkness. My wife lay under a light blanket, breathing noiselessly. Her eyes, which had looked at me so many times, were closed and still. There was a light scent of her perfume.

"I stayed there in the room as the men, practiced as they were, approached the bed. One took the syringe in hand and, just as she shifted a little, injected her with a tranquilizer. My ego pounded inside of me. It screamed and raged, because now it had something to scream and rage for. But I had already gone past it, I had become too wide for it. 'They,' my ego screamed inside me, 'are raping her with that needle. You brought these men here to rape your wife, your Malena, our Malena — to throw her away like garbage because she knows the truth! The truth —' and I shut the ego up and buried it beneath the mountains.

"One of the men lifted my drugged wife out of the bed like she was his bride. Her white silk nightgown swept to his knees. One of her arms dropped away from her body. The man was gentle and professional but still I could see that deep within she was fighting, she was scratching and cursing, willing to kill herself from the effort. As the man turned with Malena in his arms, as I stood there dressed in a weekend suit, waiting for them to take her, I saw her gain ground in her fight against the tranquilizer as she opened her eyes slightly and looked immediately at me. In the half-millimeter of dark light that was in her eyes I saw more sorrow than had accumulated in the hearts of women over the last century. I saw fury and anguish so mixed that they had become something new, something no living human had ever expressed. I saw her falling into a deep nightmare. I saw her surpass herself. I saw the abyss.

"Any other man, even a murderer, even a human creature that could barely be called Man, would have stopped them or would have at least hesitated, told them to put her back in bed, close the shades, cover her and let her think the thing was a dream. But I turned aside and coughed, and straightened my tie.

"They walked with her out the door. The children, still sleeping and unaware, would be sent off to relatives. The businesses were already divided and frustrated investors were signing documents.

"I watched the children jump excitedly into cars

after they woke and dressed. They didn't know they wouldn't be coming back and that their mother had been carted off.

"The house was empty and dark by noon. I would be the last to leave what I'd built. I turned to the empty entrance hall and looked around at the silence of the still objects with a sense of envy. The arrogant objects that had no desire — not even a desire to mock me. I turned, locked the door and left."

The man on Spinoza Street stopped talking for a moment and looked off into no particular place, with no real emotion showing on his face. Throughout the story I questioned whether this could be real or if it was just an intricate and aimless lie. I didn't know what to say.

"Did—is—do you know where she is now?" I asked after a few moments of silence.

"Who?" he asked.

"Your wife."

"Ah. Her. She's inside me, here," he said pointing four curled fingers to the center of his chest. "Burning me, freezing me, making me pay for it."

"But where is she...physically?"

"Physically? I don't know. Maybe still in the

institution I put her in. Maybe back in the old house. Maybe in the ground. It doesn't matter where she is physically. She was lost from herself that morning. I made her into a thing. A thing doesn't care where it is."

"But you still didn't tell me how you got here — or why."

"Look. Look around you. All this human flesh walking around, making noises by friction, making noises about the noises. Nothing is any different than anything else.

"I wandered through as many different places as you can imagine. I staggered through deserts, tundras, ice caps, jungles, forests. I broke bones, ate worms and dirt, slept through nights that chilled fur-covered animals to death and drove my suffering deeper, and deeper, and it always came to the same place: the surface. My hunger, my cold, my sickness were the simplest things in the world — physical suffering — just hunger and sickness and cold. Nothing more.

"But then I found one place more terrifying than all the rest combined: The city. Here, I have all I need. I am warm, I get enough money for food and I can even see a doctor if I want. Before, in all the sinister places of the world, my life was threatened but my existence secure. Here, here in this city, in this comfortable abomination of concrete and steel, of these pleasant cafes, of the restaurants and society, is where I truly learned."

"What?" I whispered quietly, fearfully. The man turned his head slightly and looked into my eyes for the first time in the whole conversation.

"I learned," he said, "that I am crazy."

"And…" I whispered.

"That I did what I thought I could never do: sin. I sinned so that I could conquer myself through repentance. So I could suffer infinitely until the infinite stopped and I could rise to God's height. But the infinite is infinite, it stops where God starts.

"I stand here and suffer in a way that makes me think this place is actually hell — look at it — those trees, those horrific things, this stone, don't you see it? Don't you hear it?" he said, rising up as if his legs were growing. "Don't you hear it?"

"What?" I said, trembling.

"The cries. The cries and calls of a lost life. Of a life that was stolen and destroyed."

"Malena's?"

"My own!" he screamed, slamming his fist on his garbage can.

There was silence and darkness. I felt like I could

hear the trees breathing in their sleep. Everything froze in place, including the moon, until a bat made one of their rare squealing noises.

"Phhh. You. You un. We go forra dell. You un," he muttered as he withdrew into the veil of the ficus tree shadow and became silent.

I put my hand into my pocket and felt the absence of my twenty shekels. Uneasily, nervously, I looked up at the dark trees, the flitting bats and the bruised sky of Spinoza Street and thought to myself that I should have taken my ordinary route home.

White Hair Woman

"That great pressure building inside of me. That great pressure." She said it as if in answer to a question, but there was no question. She looked away with a face suntanned by the exposure of a thousand days. She was naked to the chest, sitting on the steps of a closed-up bank with just some strange wrap of cloth covering her breasts. It was her hair bursting from her head in white electric strands that revealed the most, that revealed "the great pressure" was an answer to any inevitable question about the mass of white hair.

She was a witch of the streets, Tel Aviv's silent sorceress, never allowing herself to be seen in the presence of another person, never crawling around the city like the absurd Georgian drunks, never asking, never smiling, never smoking. The only place she could reliably be seen was in the city library where out of all the blurred heads bowed over tables only one face, one giant upward-dripping stalactite of hair would call out from the studious namelessness of the room. There she was — the silent, friendless, urban witch. A woman who belonged outcast in the forests of Poland or Hungary sitting here mumbling as she read from a book in one of the few air-conditioned libraries of the Middle East.

She spoke the first words about the pressure before I had said anything. She then looked around, perched on the stairs, looked up through the sunlight and past the traffic, through me, off to some distance. I wasn't sure she realized I was still there, that I was ever there, until she looked at me and said, "What do you want?" I told her I wanted to introduce myself.

"No," she said, turning her head away. "That's not what you want. You're one of *them*."

"Who?"

"Men." She spat the word out like it was a ball of vituperation.

She stood up and walked behind the sheet of plywood that shuttered the entrance to the abandoned bank. Someone had painted the word "homeless" backwards on the wood. She burrowed in some invisible corner for a little while and came back wearing a loose sweater with a wide neck. Her hair stood on end like a giant fern sitting on her head. She held two or three plastic bags, all of them full of useless things.

"*Nu?*" she said. She must have noticed the helpless look on my face. "Are you coming or not?" and started walking down the steps.

It became clear we were heading for the library. When we got there the security guard smiled as the old woman with white hair breezed past him. In the main reading room the moody and erratic stacks of the Tel Aviv library stood looking a little defensive and a little arrogant. With all her bags in hand, the white-haired woman disappeared between the shelves. I looked around to see if anyone had recognized her, but within seconds she had returned, arms loaded with books of different sizes and colors, which she slapped down on the table.

"Nu?" she said as she cracked the first book and began to flip through the pages. "Are you going to sit?" I sat. "What do you want?" she repeated.

I was again caught off guard. "I want to know—"

"You want to know, he says. They all want to

know, they say. What do you want to know?"

"I want to know who you are."

"Idiot," she said in a huff and flipped the page of the book.

She continued to read as I watched her, saw her almost smooth hands, the holes in her clothes, the decades of grime, the harshness of the lines beaten onto her face, sag in the shoulders, and utter lack of anything like joy, happiness, or peace on her person. But then the hair contradicted everything — the wild coils, the rivulets, the soft strands by her ears, the wisps at the neck — and the white-whiteness, not a dinge of gray or a faded eggshell shading. Not even a remnant strand of black. Just the white whiteness of innocence, the blank white of trauma.

"Here. Here," she finally said, and pinned a page down with her forefinger. "You see it?"

"See what?"

"Don't be a stupid idiot. It…it's there." I saw a page of text with the heading "The Later Voyages." There was an archaic map on the facing page with a subtitle that said, "Vespucci: Major Expeditions." She looked over at me, maybe for the first time since we sat in the library, and stared at me like a teacher waiting for an answer.

"It's him," she said. "Right there, his footprints."

I sat there staring at her like the idiot she took me for. She turned back disdainfully, read from the book with mumbling lips, closed it, and tossed it aside. I saw the title, *The Italian Explorers*.

She grabbed the next one from the pile — a dense, fat tome — and cracked the cover to reveal strings of esoteric formulas and trees of mathematical equations. She huffed and closed the book immediately. The next book she opened she dove into. She devoured it, nodding, bouncing between pages. "He's here. He's somewhere here. He left me marks." She read on and on, making remarks and comments, and then finally tossed the book aside, as if it had meant nothing.

She took two more books and did much of the same thing, sometimes finding signs of "him" and sometimes not. And then, after two or three hours, she stood up. I stood also. She looked at me with excited eyes and asked me, "Do you have a message from him?"

"From who?"

"Oh yes, oh yes, you're the imbecile, I forgot. Sit, sit." We sat back down. "You need to know that he is my husband, Yuval Aluf. He loves me, and of course I love him, which is why I have to find him. He was taken a long time ago, but left signs for me to follow and find him."

"He wrote the signs in the books?"

She sighed with exasperation. "Of course not, he would never write in a book."

"Then where are the signs?"

"In the world, all over the world. The books transmit them."

"I see," I said.

"No. You don't."

It was weeks later when I remembered the name. Yuval Aluf. I'd thought about her endlessly but I never remembered the name. When I finally did I didn't miss a beat. I found the name in the phone book, where the man's number and address were listed. I picked up the phone to call him but asked myself what I would say. And then I thought that even if I had something to say he would probably just hang up. It seemed better to at least have a door slammed in my face.

An old man opened the door and looked at me kindly but skeptically. "Yes?" he said.

I stammered in response. What could I say? An old, white-haired witch mentioned your name a few days ago? Or, introduce myself as — as what? I waited, looking at him and he waited looking at me, clutching the door.

"This is going to sound strange."

A tired smile crept up to his face. His eyebrows shrugged. "Not as strange as you think. Come in. Tea?" he asked, as he shuffled into the apartment behind me.

"No thanks, I—¨

"Take the tea. It makes it less awkward."

While he clattered around in the kitchen, I slowly paced around the living room. It was the ordinary living space of an old person — frozen somewhere in the mid-1970s, with framed photos of him, a wife, a family, and a few decorative relics standing on the countertops. It was nothing more, and nothing less, than a den of loneliness, a place where a man ends.

He came back into the room with two mismatched cups. He gave me one and sat down in an armchair. I sat across from him on a sofa.

"Let me save you — and me, too — some trouble. You saw her. You had the courage, or maybe it's audacity, to speak to her. She told you strange and mysterious things about searching through history, or the world, or the cosmos — I never quite understood which — and the only bit of tangible, sane reality that came up was me, or my name. Sound about right?"

"Actually, I'm here from the tax authority about some money you owe," I said. He paused for a second, looked confused, but then realized the joke.

"Ah, this one has a sense of humor. That's refreshing, at least." He smiled gently. I sipped my tea, which was bitter.

"I'm sorry…yes, you're right. All that happened, more or less. And now, I just want to know —"

"Yes, you want to know. They all want to know. Well, she perhaps told you we loved each other."

"Yes, she did."

"And that I was her husband."

"That too."

"Well, we were in love, but I was never her husband. It was a long time ago. You won't understand this since you haven't yet experienced time like that, but there gets a point where the past becomes meaningless. Everyone in it is dead, and all you want is for the past to die with them, so you can continue to live — even if it's only to die.

"Well," he said, looking down at the cup of tea he held, "I'm afforded no such luxury. The past comes back every few months or years — years if I'm lucky — in the form of people like you. I'm sorry to say it but every time, including this time, I hope it will be death standing there, instead of another messenger. But never mind." He sipped his tea.

"Do you know who she was?" he asked me.

"No, I have no idea."

"They never do. She was Israel's brightest star, in her day. Easily the most beautiful woman in the country. It was something generally agreed upon, like which was the best soccer team, or the most fertile region. She was an actress, not the most famous, yet, but very well known. The thing was that aside from her beauty, her talent was astounding. It literally flowed out of her. And then there was one other thing: her hair. Bright, wild orange, red, honeysuckle, gold — a million other words that couldn't do it justice. To me it always looked like the color of citrus fruit, but the most famous comment made about it — and from a film critic, no less — was that it was the color the Burning Bush must have had.

"We fell in love by accident. I was no one, a 'flyboy' in the air force, but not even a pilot. A mechanical chief. We met and — ach, never mind that, it's not important." He began to fill with emotion and seemed to be on the brink of being overcome.

"To make a very long story short," he went on, "we were in love, and it didn't work out, and after that she must have become ill."

I sat there a little shocked. That was it? "It didn't work out"?

"What do you mean, 'it didn't work out'?" I asked. "You loved her, right?"

"Yes."

"And she loved you?"

"Completely."

"So what was the problem?"

He sighed. "It was a very simple one, but painful. I loved someone else."

"More than you loved her."

"In a different way. But yes, ultimately more."

I was embarrassed to ask, hesitant to push him too far, to insult him, or to cause him to close up and leave me sunk with the mystery. But I was too far along to stop, too close to something I wanted to know, and felt I had to at least look around the next corner.

"But, what was different?" I asked.

He sighed again, with his hand on his forehead. "I might as well tell you. You might as well know. There are different kinds of loves. Yes, you nod your head — you know. But you don't know. I'm not talking about the love for your grandma versus the love for your girlfriend. I'm talking only about romantic love. I know the idea of it coming from my mouth, the words as wrinkled as my skin, the way I look, all seems faint, or ridiculous or, even worse, quaint," he said, with his eyes closed in thought. "But if you want to understand this, don't try to think to yourself that I was also once young. Think to yourself that I was once you.

"Anyways, you'll discover it, but now I'm going to give you one of the bitter secrets that we, the old, generally agree not to give, or are too tired to care about giving. Her love was like fire, constantly occurring but never there. A process, not a thing. It's not that it could burn me and so I was afraid of it, that's only a cliché. It's that there was nothing to grab, to hold onto, to build with. And my wife, the woman I married, was more than just love, though her love was less. She was a person, which meant that she could build a life with me, support me as I supported her, and, of course, give me children."

"And she — the other — couldn't do that?"

"No. But even if she could, physically, how could she, let's say, spiritually? What can fire rear, what can it raise, except more fire? What can it create, except destruction?"

"What about warmth?"

"Ach, no. Blankets provide warmth. A mother provides warmth. Never mind. It was all meant to be. My wife is my wife. She's dead now, she doesn't exist, and still she is my wife. How could she ever not have been, despite the love of another woman, even if that love had the power to destroy Jerusalem."

We sat in silence. The old man looking at his old cup, the room around him, his world, passing into decay.

"So you decided on love, you chose your love."

"Yes."

"And…"

"And I married that woman and lived my life."

"But what happened to her?"

He paused for a second as if someone had suddenly whispered something in his ear, a word of advice, or a reminder. He inhaled deeply as if he was breathing in time. He pushed his glasses on his nose and let his hand linger there for half a second, tired, exhausted as only a person who has lived his lot can be exhausted. And he looked back at me, sitting there in my youth, eager, digging into a story that was his life, exhuming a part of him which had died.

"Listen to me," he said, "I'm older than you. I've lived many lives and I now understand one or two things. Vanity, it's all vanity. It's all a vicious, endless wind. Some people see that, and some people don't."

I looked at him quietly. The words sounded true and wise but meant nothing real to me.

"Look," he said impatiently, "I don't know what happened. I wasn't there. I had left. They said, though, they said that one day she left a friend after meeting at a cafe, and she was beautiful as ever, and her face rubbed raw by the tears, but they said — they all said it — that her hair was brighter, they said 'stronger,' than it ever had been. No one knows how long she was there, in her apartment shut away, or what she did there. But she came out weeks, or maybe even months later, and her hair was white. I saw her after that once, from a distance, walking around like she was on another planet. And that's the last time I saw her, though unfortunately — excuse me — not the last time I heard from her."

"And now?"

"Now there is no now. There is morning and day and night in a cycle. There is only a now when they — you — come knocking."

"How many of...me have there been?"

"Who knows. I never counted. Fifteen? Twenty? Fifty? Though maybe I'm just senile and you're the first," he smiled. "And maybe you're the last."

We sat in silence for a few minutes. I finished my tea and began to get up to thank him and say goodbye, but he stopped me.

"Now listen. I told many of them to drop it — for their own sake. You seem like a nice boy, and you are certainly young. When young people or middle-aged people tell you you've got your whole life in front of you, it doesn't mean anything, they're just farting. But when someone like me says it, after everything, after feeling this old thing lodged in my chest for fifty years like a rotting lemon, when *I* say you have your whole life in front of you, it means something. Did you hear me? You have your whole life in front of you. Live your life, step into it, accept it, stop with this nonsense." He paused and looked out the window then looked back at me.

"It's romantic to think about a black hole, even to look at it, but if you start to approach it, it sucks you in. There is no mystery here. Just a woman neither of us know and who is sick. So go, look, but then leave it, and more than anything, don't take it as a symbol."

I looked at him for a second and then thanked him. I stood and began to walk out but stopped, turned to him and without thinking asked him, "If I see her again, should I tell her anything from you?"

A spark of sorrow burst into his eyes. It was so dark that had he been a slightly younger man I would have taken it for rage. He stood there frozen as if he was holding his breath. He didn't look at me. He looked past me. "Tell her," he said, "tell her: Her name is Earth, and of no worth, are all her ways."

With his hand on the edge of the door his eyes returned to him, he exhaled, and became old again. He looked at me one last time and said goodbye.

Yuval Aluf and the white-haired woman. For months I tried to take Aluf's advice to stay away from what he called the back hole, to leave it alone, and try to live my life as if it were my own. But I couldn't. The two were there with me, he fading away in his room, and she floating around the city invisibly, with her white hair following after.

It was a Friday that I got out of bed wanting to exhaust the day. I opened the weekend paper and read the news, glanced at the sports and weather and finally came to the obituaries where Yuval Aluf was the first death listed. I stared at the name and the meaningless sequence of letters and words — twenty-five, fifty, or one hundred characters of a life, and was overcome by sadness. I wondered if I actually had ended up being the last of the messengers, as he called us.

I sat and smoked, and with an unbearable, sopping heaviness, let the weekend pass around me. When Sunday came I woke up and without thinking walked straight to the main library. And of course, there she was, the center of the room, attracting every particle of light.

She looked up and seemed to recognize me. She pulled the chair next to her away from the table. I walked over and sat down. She still had her finger on a page of the book she was scouring. I didn't bother to look at the page or at the book's title. I looked at her, and she looked at me.

"You know," she said with her face still bowed to the page. Then she slowly turned to look at me. She studied my face without embarrassment, without the need to hide her action behind a convention. I allowed her to do it, as if she was doing something that exceeded me, something that had to be done for my own sake. I stayed quiet but looked back at her. Everything about her was still the same, the weatherworn skin, the high cheekbones, the grasping, suspicious eyes, and the burst of white hair.

The old man was right. It was a black hole I was staring into, much more so than anything found in the recesses of the sky. Here in the library the woman sat, contradicting herself with every breath and blink, an animal peering into the eternal, needing so much more than her physical needs that she had swallowed herself in humanness.

An impulse halfway between thought and emotion, or a mixture of the two, began to form in me, and I felt that as it rose to the surface it would be the one true thing I had acquired in my twenty-some years of living. It began in my chest, preceded by smaller bubbles of memory which flashed in my brain as sensation. And then the force of it began to escape my chest cavity, flew up into my throat where it felt like a groan, and just as that notion entered my brain, where it could have been viewed in full, she interrupted me, saying in her parchment voice, "You know. Tell me what you know."

I looked down at the table, concentrating to remember the exact words Aluf had given me for her. Slowly, without any modulation of my voice, without making an effort to be sure that she'd hear me, I told her the three lines of the message.

She looked at me with her finger still holding her place, and looked back at the book she was reading. Slowly and ponderously she lifted her finger, paused with it in the air, and then dropped it down onto the page. I saw the words I said to her printed in the middle of a page of Hebrew poems. But she, the woman with white hair, wasn't looking at those three lines. She was mumbling and reciting the lines directly beneath them: "How I have come, to hate this life! How bad its ways now seem."

I shook myself out of the trance and saw her sitting there, not a banshee, not a black hole, not a lost love. A woman. I got up to leave. I found myself sweating. But as I stood she put her hand on my arm to stop me. "He's come back," she said.

She turned back to look at the book. But as she looked down, all the strands and coils of hair swept along a second afterward, as if unconnected to her head. With the white mass hanging there above her, with her lips mumbling and her eyes unseeing, she traced the flow of words. And when she came to its end, she turned the page.

Mother, Father, Child

A couple strolled up to the cafe on a grim day. It had rained a few hours before but nobody minded because the city had been dry and needed the water. The woman, youngish and a little heavyset, was pushing a stroller draped by plastic to keep out the cold. Through the wrinkles of the plastic a little body, made fuzzy by the covering, was seen lying in a still sleep.

The man, handsome and also young, sat first. The mother positioned the stroller gingerly, not wanting to wake her child. Neither of the parents was beautiful, nor was there anything extraordinary about them as a couple. But in a city full of the vanity of couplehood, where young beautiful people parade around with their babies in expensive strollers as if on display, the simplicity of the two gave something warm and familiar, as if from a book, especially on the day that was narrowed by the cold.

The mother found her seat and repositioned the stroller so that she'd be better able to tend to her child if she had to. The young father took a menu, pushing a strand of dark European-looking hair away from his glasses. The mother quietly unsnapped the clasps that held the plastic to the stroller to give the child some air. As she removed the covering completely they both looked: and they saw there their child sleeping quietly, in total peace, with a little green hat on his head.

A waitress approached to take their order. They didn't understand her. She offered to bring them a menu "in English," but she offered it in a language they didn't know. They were immigrants — but not the immigrants of other centuries who came poor and hungry through disease-ridden journeys, but ones of today who are educated, maybe with a little money and even some ideology.

They asked questions in short, simple sentences about the food. Soup, they wanted. And she understood: the sweet potato soup is excellent. She recommends it, especially on a day like this, and she smiles.

As the waitress walks away, the mother leans closer to her boy. She's anxious to stroke his face or maybe rub a little sleeping finger but she doesn't want to wake him so she restrains herself. The father looks on with his knees bent, his hands thrust deep into his jacket pockets and his ankles crossed under his chair.

They speak to each other in normal tones. She pushes a strand of hair behind her ear, girlishly, reminding him perhaps of when they first knew each other in some Spanish-speaking country. When he began to date her it was because he found something in her face — something pretty, something that looked prettier to him because she wore a perfume, or maybe it was something more complicated than perfume, that smelled like no other girl he'd touched.

Their early romance was tied to the rituals of an earlier time. It was something Spanish, with innocent walks along a waterfront. But there was no contradiction with the sex that came later in the night (and in the morning); no embarrassment at their passion. Like the other women of that city, she would get up in the morning still naked, with equal unconcern for the nakedness of her body and what elsewhere might be called flaws, to open the wooden shutters and lean out over the sill.

The father gazed at the sky, not so much thinking about his former love as feeling the thought of her, when the cafe waitress returned with a large white bowl of soup in her hand, edging past the small kumquat tree planted in an oversized white pot.

The waitress left and the parents were about to take the first spoonful of hot soup when the sleeping son in the stroller gave a cough. Both the mother and the father paused and looked. He coughed again, lightly, and then again. His small chest, which had been raised slightly by the cough, rested back into the stroller, and the father again looked at the sky. The child seemed to be lolling back into his sleep. But then he coughed again. And this time, as his cheeks puffed and his throat cleared itself of whatever was caught there, his eyes opened and he looked around.

The father gently edged the napkin and spoon away from himself to make some room, even though there was plenty of space on the table. As he shifted in his chair the mother stirred a glass of milk and muesli and the child whimpered. She offered him a spoonful of food which he took and then she licked the remnants off the spoon and dipped it back into the glass. The child whimpered again, sputtering his cries like his cough. As the father was lifting his spoon from the bowl of soup the whimpers quickly gathered momentum and before either the father or the mother had time to prevent it, whole cries were erupting from the child.

She tried to offer him more food but with every offer the cries grew louder and more furious until, with mucus spread across his face, the boy was screaming in the stroller. Quickly, the mother rose and pushed him away to take him for a walk around the block.

The young father sat calmly in front of the soup as the mother and child disappeared around a corner. He bent over the soup in silence and began to eat a little. After a few spoonfuls he stopped and, with his knuckles resting on his thighs, he looked in the direction that the two had gone. He sat there staring for a little while and then again bent over the bowl of soup and ate. Below him his ankles were still patiently crossed.

The mother soon returned with the boy, who was calmer. But the moment she sat down the screaming began again. This time it was rage. He twisted against the buckle of the stroller, slamming his little head against the seat and kicking his feet. The more the mother tried to placate him, the harder he screamed. It was clear that he blamed them, even if he couldn't express it, for his rage and dissatisfaction. And it was clear from the mother's doting and the father's stillness that the parents had come to accept the indictment.

Neither of the two spoke. She took a quick bite of the soup and a sip of water and, again pushing a curl of hair behind the ear, she stood to walk the boy around the corner. She didn't look at her husband as she rose, and he didn't look at her. She tended to the child and he kept his eyes downward and bent over the soup.

As the mother pushed on, the boy struggled against the stroller as if he was fighting for his life. His little fists pounded its sides and his feet battered the footrest. As they walked farther away, the boy ripped the green hat from his head and ejected it from the stroller. The mother stooped to pick it up and left it clenched in her hand as she continued to push.

The father stayed there with his ankles crossed, in decent shoes and his nice European-styled hair falling over his forehead. He sat there in complete silence, young but hunched, no longer eating but simply gazing downward as he heard the enraged shrieks of grief and anger, directed at least in part towards him, coming from somewhere down the block.

Above him the grey clouds had cleared to reveal a nearly transparent blue sky, the color of which the city had not seen for a full year. But he did not look up again to see it. He sat there stooped, his eyes and his ears filled with the still audible cries of violation and hatred being emitted by his child. Slowly, he looked down at the table. And though he was overwhelmed by a desire to take the white bowl and fling it against a pane of glass, he lifted the spoon and carried on eating his soup.

On Allenby

On Allenby Street in the city of Tel Aviv, that city that looks like a smattering of barnacle spread across the bottom of a boat, on Allenby Street, which was once the great street where the Mugrabi Cinema sat in a monument of a building, a cube edifice that was a kind of Masonic lodge for the city's elite, in that city, on Allenby Street, where today the sidewalks are lined with Slavics selling sex, Israeli barmen in-gathering Filipino workers desperate for drink and escape, where the restaurants boast foods of dubious origin, where the road has become a throat vomiting the city's insides out into the sea at Beit Ha'Opera, on that street, sat Shlomi the beggar.

Shlomi sat on the naked sidewalk, maybe with a thin spread of cardboard under him, his arm bleeding perpetually into a yellowing bandage, his pant legs rolled up to show the horror of scaly scabs covering his legs, the hand of his bad arm pressed to his heart in protection of the extremity and in self-solace of the organ, and his good hand thrust out to the passing city, asking, imploring — begging.

Sometimes a stranger would deposit a few agurot, a shekel or two, even a five-shekel coin if it was a holiday. But even for a beggar it was a pitiful living. It wounded his beggar's pride as the pride of a lawyer or doctor — a professional pride — gets wounded when underpaid. But Shlomi sat there oozing himself out of his legs, waiting each day until just after sundown to roll down the pant legs, as the factory boss rolls down his shirtsleeves, fold up his cardboard pad, count the earnings, and go home.

Where was his home? It's enough that it was, that it existed in some sense, and it's beyond the scale of this minor history to follow him into his only place of privacy. So for now we'll leave him be.

Across the street, on Allenby Street, sat Yossi-Mendel, long just Mendel. Years ago Mendel had been just Yossi and in his little town in the south, and with a business that was small but steady, Yossi was even looked upon with some admiration. Mendel, obviously, was not. Even as a beggar he felt himself slipshod sitting on Allenby Street, not on the side of the even numbers but on the odd. And being superstitious as a beggar, Mendel thought his situation as unlucky as left-handedness.

Mendel, moreover, was forced to sit there under the beating sun, choking on bus fumes, being knocked by hurrying knees, watching as his neighbor, his adversary, Shlomi, took in what seemed to Mendel of the Odd Numbers to be a killing. He could see the sick dull glint of a muddy gold reflect off the dropping agurot, the pure silver shine of the shekel, the two-shekel, the five-shekel pieces, and, outrage upon outrage, the heavy drop of light produced by a falling ten-shekel coin.

"Some people have it all," Mendel jealously thought to himself as he watched Shlomi peel a scab off his bloody leg before rolling down his pant legs one early sunset evening.

One day, not much later, Mendel arrived at "the office," spread out his cardboard pad, endured the splintering of arthritic pain shooting through his body as he lowered himself to the ground, suppressed the pangs of hunger in his belly and the *hamsin* of thirst in his throat, and was shocked by the sight he saw.

Someone had dropped a shekel into Shlomi's box. But it wasn't just that, because a moment later there was another, and then someone else another, and twenty minutes later another. The even numbers were indisputably more lucrative, of course, but this! He looked, and looked, ignored his own earnings, sweated bullets from the intensity of thought, and then in one moment, just as a genius inventor solves his greatest problem in an instant of almost idiotic effortlessness, Mendel understood: Shlomi, he saw, was wearing a kippah. He felt that strange feeling, which anyone with a sense of upward ambition has felt, of a jealous hatred, almost a disgust, fluidly mixed with admiration. Why had he never thought of this?

The next day, Mendel arrived on Allenby Street wearing a kippah. But Mendel had once run a small but stable business and understood that to just match a competitor is to lose to a competitor. So Mendel wore a kippah, black, large and visible, and below the black kippah he had the hair around his ears pushed forward as peyas.

Shlomi of the Even Numbers was having a good day — or at least a good morning. The previous day business had been booming and all because of a kippah. "Who ever thought that religion could be such a wonderful thing?" he thought to himself. And this was easy street, the high life: no kneeling on the pavement like a prostrate Moslem, no wailing for the scruples of Am Yisrael, no painstaking hermeneutics translating his begging signs into English, Russian, or French. Just a holy rag on his head and the bounty of the Lord in his box.

He settled down into his spot, more hopeful than on the day before Yom Kippur, and he looked up, ready to bless his first customer with health and all good things from God, and was outraged. Mendel was sitting there Indian-style, moving this way then that, taking silver from this one, bronze from that — and then, then, adding insult to injury, sticking dirty fingers in his hopeful eye, he watched as a young man (a tourist, but never mind), handed him a bill — paper money. A week of Shlomi's work in the space of Mendel's minute.

His first reaction, like anyone who's been bested in business, was to confrontation. He began rolling his pant legs down and was getting up to trudge across the street and give that worthless Mendel a "what-for," to protect and patent his own innovation, to secure his future! But Shlomi of the Even Numbers thought better. "Mendel is stubborn as a corpse," he thought to himself. "God Himself couldn't compel him to take that kippah off his head." Shlomi knew what he had to do. So, he rolled his pant legs back up, changed his beggar's box for the panhandler's cup, and started working as no veteran beggar likes to work. But it had to be.

Ten thousand miles away, a young rabbi was carefully folding his clothes: his extra black coat, his three pairs of black pants, his black socks, and his seven white shirts. Lastly, he lifted his hat, handling it with the tips of his fingers lightly touching the brim, and lowered it into the hatbox marked *Miller's Hats, Monsey, New York*, from which it came. Young Rabbi Sirkin's young wife, Sara, watched him tenderly and a little ironically. "A funny man to be packing his own bags," she thought to herself. "But a good man," she again thought, this time switching into her mother's Yiddish.

Rabbi Sirkin had no time for reminiscence. He still had to figure out how the Chumash and the Tanya would fit into his book bag, and he had to make sure the taxi was on its way, and that his flight was on time, and the hotel confirmed…and — and Rabbi Sirkin was going to the Holy Land.

There in the Holy Land, in the Land of Milk and Honey, of lutes and lyres, prophets and biblically rolling hills, Shlomi walked in the dawn past a whore still lingering in the murky hopes of the night. He smiled an inventor's smile. The whore looked at him, her eyes bleary, her belly slack in relief after several hours of being sucked into her spine, and said, "Good morning, Rav." The "Rav" Shlomi nodded to her gravely, in spite of the sly grin on his face.

He could see it all play out — how he would sit, how the coins would drop, how shocked, routed, defeated and tortured would be his opponent, Mendel. Maybe that Odd Numbered beggar would give up, leave Allenby, cross over to the tundra of Florentine, or even give up the ghost altogether. And then Mendel would take off that damn kippah!

Shlomi (of the Even Numbers) sat himself down on his cardboard slip, the picture of a Jewish Buddha with a self-contented smile on his lips, and in place of beads and a purple belly, tzittzis covering his chest, peyas draped around his ears, a kippah on his head, and over the kippah a dowdy, beaten-up black hat, his pant legs rolled down (mindful of his modesty), a tallis draped around his shoulders, and, to top it all off, a small unframed picture of Schneersohn, the

Rebbe, sitting by his feet.

Rav Shlomi had a good day — a very good day. But it would only be a day. Mendel was once Yossi, and Yossi was once a businessman, and the next day, after recovering from the scandalizing shock he received upon seeing the seated Rav Shlomi adorned as if hands had been laid, Mendel returned dressed with meticulousness, no two fabrics blended, not with a photo of the controversial Schneersohn but, instead, two pictures, one of Ovadia Yosef and one of the Ashkenaz Rav Metzger laying at his feet. But then Mendel, proud to once again have "Yossi" in his life, did what to Shlomi was literally unthinkable. He began to pray.

When the Young Rabbi Sirkin arrived at Ben Gurion airport he had stars in his eyes. It, of course, was not the first time had been in Israel, but it was the first time he was in Israel as a rabbi — the first time, that is, he was in the Land not as a ward of Yeshiva Yom Tov.

Israel, however, wrestling not just with God but with His holy men as well, was sure to quickly remove those stars from Sirkin's eyes and put them back in the sky, where they belong. The taxi driver from the airport charged him, first of all, the double rate and then yelled in some bizarre Sephardi dialect until Sirkin, whose first name was Jacob, was browbeaten into admitting he was the guilty party. Then his hotel informed him upon his arrival on Friday morning that he had been "upgraded" to a fourteenth-floor room ("Wow, thank you," he said in English), but that the "Shabbat elevator" — meaning, the elevator — had broken down. But, he was told, he was still free to use the stairs, and his "thank-you" turned around and slapped him. And that afternoon, before meeting his colleagues for Shabbos, starving after not eating for fifteen hours (the airline had mixed up the order and gave his kosher meal to an evangelical), he was laughed at three times by restaurant owners when he asked if their place was certified kosher.

And then thoughts of his Sara arose, cooking *kneidlach* in their home, and of his walks through the quiet — and clean — streets of his hometown, getting ready to go to the shul, which he knew so well, and Young Rabbi Sirkin couldn't help feeling that the Promised Land had somehow been quietly moved to Monsey. But despite it all there was salvation for the young rabbi — salvation which lay, as it sometimes does, in hunger.

He was wandering through the city ashamed of himself, feeling his smallness and infortitude compared with the great masters who had fought disease and invaders to be on the soil he now tread, who hid their sidurim and died for pieces of parchment to have the freedom he now forgot. Shame and doubt, and a secret anger at the place causing him these dangerous emotions.

But then, then, he was stopped dead in his tracks at the sight, so unlikely, so alien to the preened streets of America, that he never even thought to think it: two beggars on this ugly street sitting and facing each other and davening in their humility, shawled by the vestments of the Tradition, devoted to God, even as they suffered in the cradle of poverty.

Shlomi of the Even Numbers and Mendel of the Odd were indeed praying, moaning the Shema, the Hatzi Kaddish, the Aleinu, screeching out Lecha Dodi, no matter what day of the week or hour of the day, as they waged this war of devotional display. They were at stalemate, as the street's regular passersby had gotten used to them and could once again comfortably ignore their plight, and so the beggars' equaled innovation brought in an equally watery income. And, of course, neither was willing to give in.

Rabbi Sirkin, first time in Israel as a recognized

rabbi, wanted to weep. But he didn't. He decided, for better or worse, that he and Sara would be there — here! — where the beggars pray to God on modern streets. He was awestruck and dumbfounded. He was inspired. Sirkin forgot his hunger (such is spiritual nourishment) and decided he would do something — *do* something, that auxiliary verb so precious to young men stepping out into the world from all walks of life, whether rabbi or pornographer. But Sirkin decided he would do the right thing.

Secretly, Shlomi of the Even Numbers was on the verge of despair. He had been blessed with a creative idea, and then had been robbed of that idea — one of his very few possessions — by that capitalist, Mendel. He felt humiliated, even if he was still earning five percent more as a devotional beggar than as a regular one.

Across the street, in front of the luckless Odd Numbers, Mendel was infuriated. He has invested good money — cigarette money, food money, vodka money! — in these robes and straps, in photos of holy idiots, and he is not enjoying the kind of return on investment that the first stream of clinking coins had promised.

Both men sat there feeling like they'd never been

lower, as if things had never been worse. Shlomi of the Even Numbers thought about rolling his pant legs back up, but rolled his eyes at the effort and then was so disgusted by the general situation — tefillin box on his head, stifling black polyester suffocating his body — that he was even tempted with that kind of urge to self-destruction, which we all have felt, to abandon his territory in front of the Even Numbers and let come what may.

Mendel was in no better a position. He began to undergo the horrifying process of remembrance: of what had happened over the past weeks, of how he had come to this dirty little nook of the world in the first place, of who he used to be, and of the sad and torturous road that took him away from himself, from his town, from his family.

And then everything changed.

A hand was holding a fifty-shekel bill and a mouth was saying "How are you?" in some strange Ashkenazi intonation. Shlomi of the Even Numbers looked up, not even taking the money, and saw a sunny face under a black hat.

"Please take it," the man, Young Rabbi Sirkin, said.

Shlomi murmured an awestruck *toda*.

"Please, please. It's you who has helped me, *adoni*, you have given me strength, I should be thanking you."

Shlomi reached out to take the money just as Mendel, across the way, raised himself up, straightening his neck like an alarmed bird, pulling his eyes wide to see what was going on over there by the ridiculously fortunate Even Numbers.

Just as Shlomi was about to release a waterfall of thanks, praises, blessings, bows and whatnots, the black-hatted giver had gone and was walking across the street, passing through the traffic like a drugged man and, to Shlomi's outrage, was approaching Mendel.

Shlomi thought he could already see the tzadik's mouth saying the words, "Please…it's you who have helped me…given me strength…should be thanking you…" and Shlomi watched as Mendel made the same dumbstruck face that he himself must have worn just a few minutes before.

Then, just a moment later, he saw something even crazier than a fifty-shekel note: the tzadik and the beggar were crossing back to Allenby's Even Numbers, towards him!

"What kind of trick is this? Mendel has paid

someone to rob me again!" he thought. But a few seconds later, as the unlikely couple approached, he could see Mendel's face was as innocent and clueless as a lamb's, and he knew there was no scheme.

The tzadik spoke to both of them, his voice getting raw as he strained over the screaming buses and the shouts of store owners. But he managed to tell them that Shabbos was coming in a few hours and he wanted them to honor him by joining him at synagogue that night. They stood there — one stood, really, and one sat — and silently blinked their assent.

Young Rabbi Sirkin delivered a great sermon that night at the medium-sized Chabad synagogue in Tel Aviv. He had Shlomi and Mendel sitting on either side of him on the *bima* and spoke to the congregants about charity, tzedakah. "But more than just tzedakah," he sermonized, "and more than just faith, but the chain of mitzvah which begins in deed and passes along in deed from man to man, woman to woman, and generation to generation and constitutes the Jewish People."

Despite the unorthodoxy of making a speech of this kind in an Israeli synagogue, the crowd was wowed and all had fallen in love with the two Allenby beggars who sat there not knowing if they were going to be rewarded with goods and cash or taken to the Temple Mount to be sacrificed.

Of course, it was the former. The men were given a little room in the back of the synagogue to sleep in and so they unconsciously suffered each other's company through the night. The next day a banquet was given after Shacharis in their honor — smoked fish, rye bread, cream and wine. At the end, not a few caring wives and mothers slipped each of them a couple of coins, and the two men accepted all this wonderful fuss silently and with big eyes.

The days passed, the weeks moved on, Shlomi and Mendel stayed, were given nice new clothes to wear, one a new tallis to replace the tattered old thing he wore, the other new teffilin to substitute for the smelly set he had. They were also honored with some responsibilities — not work but mitzvoth, the one caring for Aron HaKodesh the other in charge of the Eternal Flame. All along, they were given five shekels here, ten there, sometimes a twenty, a fifty, one hundred, and once, making them drunk with its red hues, an imperious two-hundred-shekel bill.

It was a small price to have to listen to the whining

and chattering of the congregation's women who thought maybe these "men of the world," who had vagabonded, conquered such a variety of sin, could dispense worthy advice. But the best advice often lies in the telling of the problem, and so when Shlomi muttered "I will think about it," and when Mendel nodded and mumbled an almost incomprehensible restatement of the problem, the women could walk away at least relieved, feeling blessed and, of course, happy to give.

With the men it wasn't quite so simple because they, as men, held true to their manly duty: They formed factions. Sirkin of course was the beggars' benefactor and advocate, and the old, brittle (but spiny) Rav Hildescheimer was the skeptic, the social prosecutor, the spiritual bloodhound. The game went on, Sirkin proposing new adventures — now an aliyah to the Torah (neither could remember his father's name, though Shlomi made one up); now a raising of the scrolls; now a lesson in Gamatriah (easy enough for professional coin counters); and even, eventually, a leading of a prayer.

From the outside, Shlomi and Mendel were illustrious men in deep black clothes, peyas shining, pure white tallitoth, and sidurim tucked perennially underarm. For the two old street scabs, life in the synagogue was heaven: money flowing like gutter water after an Allenby rain, food available, a sleepy schedule, no heavy lifting, and wine on a clockwork basis. What a life!

One day Sirkin, who had become a rising star in the community thanks to his work with the beggars, invited them into his small temporary office in the synagogue. He stood up to greet them, sat down, and said, "Gentlemen, you are so admired here. I have spoken with some members, and despite the reasonable objections of the Tzadik Hildescheimer, we've agreed that it's time for you to move up a level."

Shlomi and Mendel sat there not knowing what he was talking about (they rarely did), but were assured that it meant, essentially, "more" and "better."

"We have been a little selfish here," Sirkin continued. "For the giver, giving feels so good, and the mitzvah of tzedakah has its own kind of wonderful thrill. But for you, the receiver, it does not feel so good, and you — strong, able men — must suffer because of it."

(At this point they really had no idea what he was talking about.)

"As you know, Rambam teaches that the highest

form of charity is not to give, but to enable." (And now the two listeners grew perplexed.)

"You deserve better — lives of your own, homes of your own, a salary of your own."

(Shlomi looked out the corner of his eye at Mendel; Mendel looked back, out the corner of his eye, at Shlomi.)

"Beginning tomorrow," Sirkin said, beaming out a smile of joyousness that would have warmed the coldest *misnagid*, "you each will have a position, and each will be properly compensated."

Neither Shlomi nor Mendel knew what this was all about, but, all the same, neither of them liked it. When, the next day, each was given a list of tasks to do — good work, noble work, easy work — they began to do it, but with a heavy doubt in their hearts.

Shlomi dropped a set of sidurim he was supposed to be stacking and looked up at Mendel as if for help but Mendel looked back at him, holding the dislocated seat of one of the synagogue's wooden chairs, which he was supposed to be cleaning. Shlomi later that day broke a *havdalah* candle in half, and Mendel chipped the glass of a donated chandelier. Needless to say, neither completed any of their tasks but, instead, created twice the amount of work that they were supposed to have done in the first place.

Sirkin merrily walked in at the end of that first day to see how things were progressing and saw the synagogue a shambles. He was confused, but seeing the placid look on the men's faces, an animal calm, a heedlessness of wrongdoing, he grew confident and rosy again, and assured the two that they would certainly do better as they learned.

"Do better at what?" Shlomi turned to Mendel after the Rav had left. Mendel shrugged his shoulders, reminding himself he was only once a businessman, and not one any longer.

Sikrin came back the next day, a little earlier this time to make sure Shlomi and Mendel were "getting the hang of things," as he'd said when he was explaining to the irate Hildescheimer faction what had happened. The synagogue was in good order when he entered, no sign of new breakages, knocked-over books, or broken chairs. He called out to Shlomi, and then to Mendel. He looked for them in the women's balcony, in the smaller chapel, in the storeroom, and the kitchen. A quiet doubt washed over Young Rabbi Sirkin that maybe the two beggars were hiding somewhere, maybe embarrassed by their mistakes, maybe nervous about making more.

When he came to their little sleeping room he was even more confused. Two black suits, two tallitoth, two sets of tefillin, two sidurim, one photo of Schneersohn, one photo of Ovadia Yosef and one of Rabbi Metzger lay on the makeshift cots, in no particular order — the clothes, prayer shawls and phylacteries laying there as if their owners had been snatched naked from under them.

That next Shabbos, Hildescheimer sat in the congregation smiling a knowing smile which Young Rabbi Sirkin strained to look away from. The wives and mothers looked at him as disappointed wives and mothers look at a once favored husband or son, and they very slightly shook their heads.

Sirkin was downcast for days. His visit to the Holy Land was coming to its end, and this is how it would end. On the final day he wandered the city, too embarrassed to go back to the synagogue of the congregation whose faith he had invested in an illusion. He stumbled down Ben Yehuda Street, past Gordon and Frishman streets, and crossed the no-man's-land onto Allenby.

Eventually, he looked up and from a short distance saw Shlomi of the Even Numbers, sitting in front of the even numbers, pant legs rolled up, legs scabbed and oozing, and Mendel of the Odd Numbers, sitting on the odd side, with one arm wrapped in dingy bandages, both of them holding their hands out as if to the sky but, from a closer distance, Sirkin could see, not to the sky but to the willingness or unwillingness of the people passing by.

Little Old Lady
With The Flowers

She walked around the city pushing a small cart with four wheels, dressed in clean dresses with bright floral prints on them, wearing old running shoes much too big for her. Her face was weathered, old, but in its own way pretty. Her eyes smiled through a few decades of hardship, her fingers trembled a little, but there still seemed to be something happy about her.

They say that near the end of life we return, as grown infants, to the cradle. The little old lady with the flowers pushed her own cradle, as she probably had for a long time. It was filled with flowers. Careful students of the city could see her sometimes picking the flowers from the city's sparse gardens. Like a bird-watcher catching a rare bird building its nest, or an anthropologist seeing a tribe in a supersecret ritual, if you were quiet enough and patient enough you could see the little old lady with the flower-print dresses and a tanned, weathered face filling her cart with flowers.

The city's only farmer, you could call her. And giving her twenty shekels for her flowers raised the smile of a harvest glow to her face, and brought the million grateful thanks of simplicity to her lips. And if she could still cry, she would.

Each night she goes home. But only very late, after pushing her cart down nighttime streets, returning glass bottles for less than a handful of valueless coins: she returns to a tiny place only God knows where; a nook in the rubble of the city.

The little old lady selling flowers — full of life's answers. A walking guidebook to the universe, older than the hills, certainly older than the city's oldest buildings. But for all the hidden answers she contains, there's only one question you, if you could meet her, could ask her: Where do you come from?

Where did she come from? Born on a beach or a moshav? Raised on rich farmland or in the shivering city? Taught the alphabet of socialism or the arithmetic of trade? It's impossible to know. Before he died, my grandfather (who, old and ripe as he was, was not older than the old lady with the flowers) asked me to sit with him on the raised wooden porch next to their small plot of forested Georgia land. A Jew from Germany settled into the genteel, memoryless, suburban South, he said to me, with his veins running freely with thought and remembrance but less so with blood, "You must ask me, you must remember. Because I find now, at my age, there's no one left to ask. They're all gone." I sat there, but I didn't know what to ask.

But with the little old lady with the flowers I know the question, but still there is no one to ask. I could follow her crisscrossing, zigzagging city miles, or I could wander around with her — as I do with a beautiful stranger — for only a few steps, and I would learn nothing. She would disappear like a small bird into a tiny, invisible nest; into some ground-floor hovel, and even if I could follow her in and ask a million questions, I would receive the only answer I've ever gotten out of her: a litany of joyous but tearful thanks for the bit of money I sometimes give her in exchange for a flower, a flow of blessings and goodwishes which tell me something about her soul but nothing about her past.

But still I imagine her, maybe as what I need to imagine her. Young, pretty, sheltered by her strength, happy, alone, walking down the street carrying packages. And later in love, married, and then a mother. And then raising those children, holding them by the hand to cross the furious streets, sitting with them at meals, wondering at their growth and intelligence. And then one by one — no, I can't talk about it, because I don't know.

One night I saw her waiting outside a supermarket, late, staring into the bright lights of the place. She stood there in her big running shoes and sagging socks, her four-wheeled cart next to her, waiting. Her eyes were eager and patient. She was waiting to exchange some bottles for an amount of money that you or I would consider no more than a burden of dirty metal in our pockets. But she waited. I had fifty shekels burning a hole in my pocket. Fifty shekels I would be happy to rid myself of, to give to her, to provide her with bread for a month. I looked at her and found myself walking in the other direction, carrying my packages. I looked over my shoulder, longing, but kept walking. I reached the end of the block and saw her in my mind, waiting, and felt the money in my pocket, and kept walking. And I didn't do the easy, obvious thing. I didn't turn back, but left her waiting there, without offering, without asking. And as light as my crime was, I felt in having committed it the potential for all the human cruelty of the ages. I felt the meanness and smallness of not acting thrown up against the backdrop of doing worse than nothing.

Who is the little old lady with the flowers? I could say she is many things. But in truth she walks around the city, real. She exceeds the narrow, shallow boundaries of this writing. She is an ocean unto herself, and like the ocean doesn't know it. She knows only her own rhythms, her waking up in the morning and putting on a flower-print dress and tying her oversized running shoes which for her are not pathetic. She pushes her cart around, selling the city's flowers to its inhabitants. She is the only one who can answer our questions and satisfy our wonder. She is the only one who knows who she is, just as she knows where she came from. And it's a knowledge she will keep, with a smile on her face and gratitude in her eyes, until she meets with death, offering him a flower, and long after.

Night of Grief

The empty streets. A wind began to blow down the boulevards and avenues and even licked its way into the alleys. The night had become gray and the streetlamps stood there looking naked, shining a light that hid nothing. The city's dust blew in circles, down Dizengoff Street around the corner of King George, and up Ben Zion to the grand boulevard of Rothschild where it dispersed and settled in the corners of pristine Bauhaus buildings.

In reality the night was mild, the weather kind. But on streets used to the sun, in love with the light, with the ficus trees grown enormous, knotted, grotesque and beautiful from a constant flow of light, where the light glittered in the air's mixture of desert sand, sea sand, and city dust, a night filled with water, a little mist, and a charcoal darkness offered little hope for light or sun. And so Tel Aviv went inside, the cats sublimated themselves and disappeared, the dogs sniffed at the air through closed shutters, and even the constant buzz of taxis with their yellow firefly lights left the streets alone.

On Dizengoff Street two young women with arms interlocked were walking in that pathetic light which made their vintage wool coats look like the last few tatters of Jewish Europe. A little further on scraps of song were drifting down the street, a familiar melody played by a flute. I knew it was him, the same man who had stood there every day for five years playing at the same tempo, in the sun, in the rain, seated, or standing, beating out the rhythm with his foot, smiling behind his flute when someone dropped a coin into his bag.

After walking the same walk for half a decade, seeing the same shops, knowing every corner of every crumbling building in Tel Aviv, I looked around and saw no alternative, not even home. So I stopped and listened, and wondered what drove the flute player out of his house to play to the streets of an empty city.

I clapped for him when he finished and we spoke for a little while. Andrei, he said his name was, told me about the school in Moscow where he'd learned music. Eventually I came to the question I'd been wanting to ask for all that time: why he stood there in the elements, without an audience, to play the same song every day. He looked surprised, even a little condescending, when he said in a milky Russian accent, "You don't know?"

He smiled as he put the flute away. "Okay, so I explain. But come to have vodka and to meet my friends. We explain. You must to meet my friends, but they not know English, they speaking Hebrew."

We walked down King George to Allenby Street and flagged down a minibus taxi. Andrei took a few coins from his night's earnings and paid the driver. I watched as the streets streamed by, the names of prophets, dead socialists, and a writer or two marking the blackened side streets. We stopped in the Shapira neighborhood where the street was also affected by the weather. But the huge kosher restaurants were still open there, and a few young Moroccans and a couple of coffee-burnt Yemenites sat smoking cigarettes in the *pitzutziot*.

Getting out of the taxi I heard a hoarse, banging shout fly down the street. I looked at Andrei, who was watching a thin female figure with long legs as she spewed a string of foul-sounding Slavic sounds. "Katerina," Andrei said. The bedraggled figure stopped across from us. She was suntanned, wearing a miniskirt and platform shoes, carrying a big purse and another larger bag with clothes hanging out of it. Still shouting in an almost motorized way, she saw Andrei and started screaming at him and shaking her fist and showing her middle finger.

"What's she saying?" I asked. He translated as she spoke.

"She's calling me piece of shit pederast, son of… eh, how you say, son of whore. And a faggot. She says also to you something," he said.

"What?"

"Eh, is not important."

Andrei waited patiently for her rant to sputter out. He then looked at her, spread his arms out and boomed a few sentences of Russian across the street. Katerina stood stunned, then spat, turned around, and hitched up her skirt to show us the full beam of her glory. Andrei laughed.

I asked what he said. "I said, 'Katerina, you princess in beggar clothe and without you Tel Aviv is be like man with broken heart.'"

"What's her story?" I asked. He shrugged

his eyebrows with that cool Russian display of indifference, frowning, pursing the lips, tilting the head, telling you that it — life — is not worth bothering too much about.

We carried on. On Etzel Street Andrei turned onto an alley cut into sharp angles by the high stone walls. Passing a harem of cats we turned onto another alley and walked up three crumbling stairs leading to a padlocked door, which he unlocked and opened. We took the stairs up a few flights and turned onto a landing where he unlocked another door. Walking in, I saw a sitting room with a few dilapidated couches. To the side was a TV on a table. Andrei walked into an adjoining room where I heard him speak Russian to someone who answered back angrily. Andrei said something again and then came walking out the room with a man behind him.

I recognized him instantly — it was Losha. For as long as I'd seen Andrei playing the flute on Dizengoff I had watched Losha a few blocks down playing the violin, his polished angular face caught in intensity as he played his own compositions. Andrei called out another name, Sergei, and a loud "*Da?*" came from a doorway connected to what looked like a kitchen. Andrei said something about vodka and the voice of Sergei answered, "*Kyehn!*" Andrei asked me to sit and I did, as did Losha. In Hebrew he said to the violinist, "We met on the street." Losha nodded.

"He wanted to know why I play the same song."

"Good question," Losha said with a fierce grin.

"Losha has different views."

"Correct views," Losha smiled.

Sergei stepped in with a bottle of vodka and a few glasses. He was taller than the other two and had frizzy black hair and thick glasses but a strong jaw.

"No fighting tonight soldier," a grinning Sergei said in Russified English. "General forbid it."

"General is an idiot," Losha responded in Hebrew.

"General is idiot, but genius," Sergei said as he poured the vodka.

"He thinks," Andrei said, laughing and gesturing to Sergei with his glass of vodka, "he plays everything, he plays the whole world."

"Mathematics is more than music," Sergei said with the defiance of a younger brother.

"Yes, yes, we know, it's life, the universe, blah

blah," Losha said, rolling his eyes.

"And our little genius knows the language of the world but still can't get a job," Andrei said smiling.

"Or a woman," Losha added, and ended the sentence with another shot of vodka.

"Oh yes, I forgot," Sergei snorted, "you two bathe in cash and use women as cushions. The life of a musician."

They were all quiet. They looked dejected and tired, more like exiles than immigrants. I broke the silence by asking if they missed their families or friends from home. Losha looked away. Andrei clasped his hands in front of him. "Our families are sleeping with the others," Sergei said with a halfhearted smile. I looked at the door where I thought the bedrooms were.

"No," Andrei said. "He means they're dead."

"Yes, they're dead. They've been dead for two hundred years. They've been eaten by worms for two hundred years," Sergei said, no longer smiling. "And they made our cemetery into apartments for oligarchs." They were quiet. Sergei's eyes were shimmering.

"What can you do," Losha said, breaking the silence.

"And your friends there?" I asked.

"We learned, I think," Andrei said, "that we never had any. That there is no such thing as friends there, only enforcers, only informers, only strangers."

"And here?"

"Even here, it's hard to sleep," Andrei said. "Vengeance is insomnia, so we have songs instead of dreams." He had another vodka. We were all quiet again. "You ask why I play the same song. I ask the same thing, and get no answer. It's just that way."

I waited quietly until I remembered something had been itching me since I'd sat down with them. "Andrei, what was it Katerina said to me?"

"It doesn't matter, she's crazy, she's czarina of her own crazy world."

"Still," I said.

He sighed. "She said you are not for this place. She said go back to America." They were looking at me with heavy eyes to see how I'd react. Maybe to see if I'd stand up and go back to America. The Russians, I saw, were starting to drift in a haze of vodka and sleepy memory. I realized it was time to go. I stood up, straightened my shirt, shook their hands and thanked them. They barely responded.

As I was opening the door I remembered

something. "I was born in Africa," I said to them. "If you see her again, tell her." They let out an exhausted laugh, and as I was closing the door I could hear Sergei shouting out a goodbye — "to the American."

Outside, the streets were still empty, but in a way no longer deserted. The weather had calmed and the layer of winter charcoal had lifted and gradually the smell of warmth, the breezes of Arabia blown into this sliver of a country, returned and took the place of emptiness.

No one was around as I continued my walk — not the Sudanese refugees that haunt the street corners by the bus station, not the whores, not the kids looking to discover things they heard whispered about. Just a dim city sleeping on its bed of crumbling buildings and blown-in sea sand.

I continued to walk, crossing the bridge at the Haganah train station, catching a glimpse of the city laid out below, at one time rising up in gleaming towers and crumbling down in stucco shacks and bones. I came to Allenby Street, so far down that it's called HaAliyah, and began to breathe again. I was the only one there, as I was so often, and felt assured by the absence.

I walked on, crossing Derekh Yafo, watching the bats swarm the hair of trees, until I saw a thin figure ahead of me. Katerina again, I thought. But as I got closer I saw it wasn't the Russian banshee. The woman ahead of me was taller, walking as if floating, not with Katerina's mannish stomp. As we neared each other I edged myself towards the street, closer to the curbside, anticipating her fear. But she continued straight on without moving, her eyes fixed not in the false stare of a woman pretending not to see a man in front of her, but in a daze. I looked down at the rotting leaves in the gutter as we were about to pass each other.

"What?" She was saying something. I turned around and saw her standing there in a tight flower-print dress, long legs bare and black hair blown across her shoulders.

"Do you want a flower?" and it was only then that I saw she was holding individually wrapped roses, selling them at three in the morning at the gangrened foot of Allenby.

She said they were twenty shekels each, a ridiculous price, but I took out the money and handed it to her, and she looked at me from her height, her eyes glaring. She moved to take the bill without looking down and grabbed my hand, encircling it, encircling me, drawing me closer.

"I have more," she said. "Come with me and I'll give you another flower." She still held onto me, looking through me, the night still descending. Ahead of me I saw the hours. I could see the rest of the endless walk. I smelled the future possibility, the decease roses and perfume decomposing on her body, and her mouth and its breath of need.

What is that other direction? Who is heartless enough to say no to that question, and let life be flesh? I looked to the left, back down the descent of Allenby towards HaAliya and thought that down there somewhere was a room up some flight of stairs, and in that room her things, another pair of shoes, makeup, clothes, a curtain or rough, colored sheet hanging on a cracked window. And in that room a bed, torn and messed but alive, and all the cheap clothes and colors of the world made meaningful by her poverty, and whatever madness fueled it. And then that madness itself, and the idea of joining with one of its bodies, of discovering the next days of the coming life.

I was closer to her now, the money was gone from my hand, she had moved that hand to the warm swell of her hip where the fishhook bone was pointing through the flowered cloth. She turned to her right, taking my hand to bring me with her, back down Allenby Street, back down there.

"I'm sorry," I said. My walk was there waiting, it couldn't be abandoned. I had to begin again — I had no choice — and I did, looking back to her once to see her standing there still trying to convince me.

The sky was opening. I walked through the softening streets thinking of all the human landmarks: the dog-eyed father and son beggars with their open hands on their laps; the bulging trombone player who couldn't play; the violin woman in sagging socks who smilingly wrenched death pangs off that sad instrument; Losha and Andrei, of course; John Dober of Spinoza Street and the woman with white hair slipping by; on and on, and never stopping. This world of others, unafraid to show themselves, never hesitating to give everything all at once. These shades.

The sky was now breaking and I could see on Dizengoff Street near Frishman the one-eyed, one-legged beggar — Tel Aviv's most horrid thing — sitting where he used to sit before he disappeared. Today you can still see the patch of grime burned onto the pavement as if he, who had sat there for at least a decade, probably more, had melted onto the street, refusing to go away. I once gave him money, dropped a few coins into his can which he shook with one hand as he propped himself up with a foot-long cane and his one leftover leg roosted underneath him, and his tangled mouth useless.

As the day started to break I could see the human thing the beggars of the city, I later learned, called "The Pile" was already there, earning money for some unknown purpose. But next to him there was an old rabbi, stooped over as if he were speaking with The Pile. I recognized the rabbi as well, the old Haredi man who, for some reason or another, walked backwards, always shuffling backwards one step at a time. At that time, he had begun to use a walker, shuffling backwards and dragging the walker with him. He would do this all over Tel Aviv, pulling the walker up Dizengoff Street and all the way back to Sheinkin, where he backed himself into one of the Haredi buildings stuck into the trendy strand like a thorn in its side.

That early day, as I said, the Backwards Rabbi had stopped by The Pile, and was stooping lower than he already was, and was saying something to him. He spoke close to the man's ear and The Pile, still shaking his can with that indifferent aggression of his, nodded once or twice, and then made some rotten sound, and the Backwards Rabbi smiled and continued on (if that can be said) down the street.

I watched it all while standing next to a bench. But I looked back at The Pile with its enormous trench coat, an eye patch over one eye, fingers bandaged, a pile of plastic bags by his side, the cane shortened to be useful only from the position of groveling on the ground. And yet this thing was asking for money! I was flooded by a need to know what this human creature was, what it could say, what kind of intention kept it upright and asking.

It hit me that this was my only chance to speak with someone who had spoken with The Pile, to ask a question and receive an answer. I took some money out of my pocket and ran up to the rabbi saying, "Rav, please, a donation for the yeshiva."

The Backwards Rabbi paused, looked up at me slowly, took the money quickly, and said, "Be healthy," and continued on with another step back.

"Excuse me Rav," I said, taking a step toward him, "I've seen that — that *man* there for five years, and I've never seen him speak to anyone before."

"Yes, well?"

"Why did he speak to you?"

"Did you hear him speak?"

"Well, no, but he responded to whatever you said."

"Ah, you think he is not human anymore. That he has no soul." I stayed quiet. "Yes he does," the Rav said, "I can tell you he does."

"What did you say?"

"That is not for you—"

"But why does he never speak to anyone else?" I said, still trying to get some kind of information.

"Them?" he said gesturing at the few people moving on the street. "They are all Forwards Rabbis, they see nothing except what is ahead of them. They see only themselves in everything."

"Is that why you walk backwards?"

"No, that is because of my leg."

He shuffled backwards, wilting, becoming more pale with each backward step. But all the time he was walking away he was still looking at me, since he had no need to look ahead of himself. And I stood there looking at him, then looking at The Pile.

"Come here," the Backwards Rabbi suddenly said. I looked up and saw he was standing in one place. "Come," he said impatiently. I walked over to him and stopped. He grabbed my sleeve and held onto it, taking his weight off of the walker, placing it on me.

"This is a big world," he said. "It is full. And everything in it is full. And we are just children—how can children carry the weight of more than the world?

"It's heavy, yes," he said, now gripping my arm and pulling down. "You want to know what was said between us, me and him?" he said, motioning with his eyes to The Pile. "It's what I've said to him for twenty years now, as I've watched him sink and slowly be swallowed by this *city*.

"You think in your mind it must be some wisdom of Kabbalah, some phrase from Tehilim. But no, no it's not.

"I pass him and though it's getting harder I bend toward him and I say to him, 'What is your name?' And sometimes he doesn't hear me, he can't hear me. And I say it again, and again, and again if I have to. I say 'What is your name?' until he tells me.

"And do you know what he tells me?" I looked at this old man in his dusty black suit, his eyes yellowed and glistening with age. "He tells me his name," the

Backwards Rabbi said to me. "Each time, his name.

"*Baruch Hashem*," the rabbi said, "his name!" His eyes sparkled with joy. "Remember this, remember it." He let go of me and shuffled backwards a step, and then another step and another, and that is how he walked away.

I stood there with my eyes dropping. I had nothing left. I walked on. It was already full light of the morning, and I was just one block from home. But there was Alex. There was Alex standing on the corner in his black rags, with bare feet, in his neighborhood where he had no home. There was Alex, who defied everything, who has no rule, no logic. Who is no story. I had never spoken to Alex, in spite of the thousand times I'd passed him on the street. Only once had I nodded to him, and he nodded back, with his clear blue eyes burning like gems in his filthy head.

I had often seen him standing outside shops with his arms crossed, sometimes conversing with the shop owner. I had seen him on a bench on Bograshov Street with a nice looking woman and her dog, listening as she explained in Russian some problem she was having. And I had once seen two young boys approach him as he walked down

Pinsker Street and offer him a little bit of money, and saw him decline it. And when one of the boys, in a kind way, insisted, Alex said no again. And when it happened again, the boy thrusting the money in his direction, he began to shout. "Get out of here!" first in Hebrew, and then in English. "Leave me, leave me!" and walked off with his bare feet padding the ground.

At the end of this long night — the beginning of the day — I saw Alex on his corner, bathing in the now hard light of the sun, asking for nothing, refusing everything, in spite of the plentitude of the city.

I walked on toward home, and it still being early, and in spite of the sunlight and the morning breeze blowing from the other side of the Mediterranean, the streets were empty. I made my way to him, I looked at him and dreaded another experience, and was anticipating the shame of ignoring him for a thousandth time in these five years. He looked up at me from his contemplation, standing with a hand pinching his lower lip, as he often was, and I looked at him. "Good morning," I said to him, and smiled lightly, as you smile to a neighbor. Alex, who without a bed had never slept, said, "Good morning," and nodded to me and looked up to the sky, no doubt wondering if he would ever sleep.

Rivkah & Rebecca

*H**e fell off his camel.*

My father would nod in my direction and say with pride and amusement that "he fell off his camel." Most of the guests who heard the regular comment of his couldn't understand it. The ones from abroad would lean forward in their chairs, trying to peer out the window in search of the camel that the shy, mostly silent boy had supposedly fallen off of. The religious and more carefully educated guests knew the story from the Torah, that when Rebecca saw Isaac for the first time she was so thunderstruck by love that she fell off her camel.

Only my father knew who had knocked me from

my saddle. Most people, including my mother, knew that it was one of them — Rivkah and Rebecca — and some family friends and cousins even had their own ideas as to exactly which. But it was my father who knew, who never spoke my secret, who sat in his armchair as if it were a throne, smiling at me graciously, slightly sarcastic with the secret but bearing the sarcasm between us, as if we were privileged with its knowledge and our irony was directed at the ignorant world outside.

Many people couldn't tell the two apart after years of knowing them. I knew which was which by the sound of their breathing. Sometimes, though, when Rebecca would lash out with the helpless rage of her sister, or when Rivkah coolly, calmly, and beautifully executed some act of cruelty that belonged to Rebecca, I'd have to shut my eyes for a second and then look at one girl and then the other to make sure each was who I thought she was.

At school they stayed bound together and indecipherable. At home or out with their family or the au pair, Clarice, they were night and day in the way they behaved, in the way they moved, the pace they talked, the way they dressed. Rebecca glided silently through everything, a little like the wind, one

minute serene and the next lashing out and raging
— but with a confidence and pride that seemed to
come from the devil. Her sister bounded around,
touching, looking, smelling, always engaging with
the world around her, always in the act of creating a
relationship with things. Rivkah wore light colors.
Her taste was intuitive and she refused to let anyone
lay out her clothes for her on the bed. Rebecca
never cared about her clothes, unless it was for some
greater purpose. Clarice had learned long ago that
commenting on Rebecca's appearance could only
bring grief to the day. So she remained silent and
winced inwardly when one of the girls' parents
showed up unexpectedly and found Rebecca in some
Bohemian drag, with her hair scraggled and a weird
smattering of makeup smeared across her face.

But at school the girls disguised themselves
in twinhood. The school uniform nullified their
difference in dress but aside from that the mutually
dulled look in the eyes, the placidness, the refusal
to involve themselves in what they saw as a petty
society had the effect of equalizing them. They had
the same friends and did the same things during the
day. But despite the generic masquerade they put
on, they were still the focus of every bit of social

curiosity and each gossip report on the campus of the American School, the institutional haven for the sons and daughters of the wealthy and important.

The girls' teachers found them to be good students. Rebecca did well in English and Hebrew; Rivkah did a little better than her twin at history and the social sciences. But it made no difference. They both sat in class with bored looks on their faces and turned in work that could prop them up above the average without deigning to be given exemplary grades by their teachers. They'd bring home graded reports to show their father, who would sit and read the reports and the red ink comments written on them by the teachers, and chuckle to himself.

But there was one night at the Simeon home which differentiated everything, setting everything apart, most of all the girls. I look back on it now and see it as the night that quickened our lives. It was the Great Shabbos dinner, the last Shabbat before Pesach, when Simeon convened the household and a few carefully chosen guests.

That night, I saw when I arrived with my parents, Rivkah had chosen to wear a shimmering pink dress and a string of pearls. At one glance I knew that she'd spent hours laying out the candidates of different dresses, comparing them, trying them on, looking at herself in the mirror, sometimes wistfully, sometimes joyfully, always with a feeling of uncertainty. I knew she probably made her final decision just hours before the beginning of the dinner, choosing the obvious choice, the light pink chiffon, the one that offered her both the risk of fuchsia and the safety of pale yellow. The one which would add color to the pearls her mother gave her and would let her feel (though she didn't know it) a few years younger at a time when she was more ready to step into the light of the world, when she was automatically the one the attention was turned to, while the other one — shy, brooding, simmering — would shelter in her shadow. But at some point everything had begun to change. Rebecca was becoming more willing to slip out into the world, if only for a few moments here and there, to show herself, especially when she saw an opportunity.

Things were beginning. The other guests were arriving. Rivkah knew it was part of her responsibility to greet the people as they walked in, and hung around the entrance hall. She loved it, shining eyes looking at her, handshakes that left the traces of perfume, questions that required no specific answer, and always a compliment, an exaggerated comment, or a rhetorical question about who that "beautiful young lady" was. She smiled through it all. She kissed every feminine cheek, shook every male hand, answered every idiotic question.

But then there was Rebecca. It was in the middle of greeting one of the guests, a famous filmmaker, when Rivkah happened to look up toward the staircase. What she saw shocked her, and she was frozen by the sight of it. It was her sister descending the great staircase. There she was, Rebecca, floating down the stairs wearing jeans and a black cashmere cardigan, elegant in her simplicity, with a necklace of carved silver in place of her sister's pearls, all of her looking casual, comfortable, cool.

I watched the whole thing unfold in movements of minutiae: Rivkah's cheeks flushed, and she was filled with a subtle fury, her fists clenched until her knuckles went white and she, I could see, had no idea what her guest, whom she was lavishing with attention a moment before, was saying to her. And Rebecca walked down the stairs, one hand lightly on the rail, looking as if her concerns were in the clouds. She couldn't care less, she seemed to say, to show, to taunt her sister with. But she cared deeply, specifically, almost passionately. The rest of the crowd, misunderstanding, ignorant of the unseen society that existed between the two girls, might have thought that she, Rebecca, was "the most natural thing in the world." Maybe — but if by "natural" they had meant spontaneous and undesigned, they couldn't have been farther from the truth.

I smiled to myself and stepped back a little to make sure I stayed unseen. Rebecca, in her almost audaciously casual clothing, her hair still damp from the shower, her body perfumed only by soap, had probably been planning this for days, maybe even weeks. I thought back to the previous few days, to every one of Rebecca's vacant looks through the car window on the way to school, to her sitting under a tree during lunch with a half-smile on her face, as every boy, girl and teacher glanced over and thought her angelic, as if she were sitting there like Sara giving thanks to the angels, and I knew — I realized as I watched her at the moment of her descending — that she'd been gently planning, plotting, focusing on this evening and, in particular, those ten seconds of walking down the stairs.

Rivkah had looked beautiful with her pink dress and pearls — and with the absence of Rebecca. And then Rebecca — with the same body, the same hands, an identical mouth, nose and eyes — walked into the room and the room no longer cared about Rivkah, and Rebecca became the only beautiful body in the room and, perhaps, in the eyes and minds of some of the guests, in the world.

Rivkah knew instantly that she'd been annihilated in that battle, since she never even knew there was a fight. But she knew that she should have known. She was outmaneuvered, outsmarted — she had been thinking only through her own eyes, seeing herself at that dinner, imagining the way all the guests would see her. She'd never stopped to think how Rebecca would see her or, worse, how Rebecca would make her look — like a ridiculous pink puff princess, like a giddy toddler in a fairy costume.

It was the only thing keeping her from bursting into tears and rage, the knowledge that there had been a skirmish and she'd been brutally routed. She had to respect her foe, to learn from it, to use its knowledge. She abruptly and coldly excused herself and ran to the bathroom. I wanted to follow her (and she probably wanted me to) but I didn't need to be there to know her reaction. And, of course, I couldn't leave the one-scene, one-woman opera, the ballet of Rebecca walking down the stairs, cunning, beautiful, and so outwardly pure that the purity seemed to turn back inward and fill her.

Despite my knowledge, I could believe in her total innocence, even as her wounded twin sat on the bathroom counter behind a locked door fuming, privately humiliated, made ridiculous for nothing, for simply existing.

The Great Shabbos dinner, which took place at the family mansion only once a year and consisted of an elite that was formed the moment it sat down at the table, was one of the major battles in the war between the twins. Though maybe it was just one of the more memorable battles, for me, since it was decisive, since it was beautiful and since I had the privilege of sitting on a quiet hill to watch it. From my view, it was momentous. The rest of the guests couldn't see a thing. They couldn't see Rivkah trembling in pain, and they couldn't see Rebecca's arrogant triumph. All these acute observers, the *branja*, the elite of Israel, celebrated professors, sensitive artists, scientists, analysts, and industrialists. And none of them could see a thing, except for the presence of Simeon's twins, pale-faced with tanzanite eyes and a stream of hair blacker than

Egypt's night. Two cute little girls, in the minds of blind observers. Two things that they would have thrown any adjective at in order to be done thinking about them, so they could return to flagellating each other with compliments.

We sat down to dinner. Rivkah reappeared with the pleats of her dress smoothed and her necklace of pearls adjusted so the clasp hung from the nape of her neck. The clothes burned her, but the feeling wouldn't last. Simeon, their towering father, the master of the house, stood at the head of the massive table laid with Scottish crystal and Spanish silver. The best bottles of wine from the Golan spotted the table and a team of servants stood waiting for the right moment to start service.

The guests at the table waited for Simeon's words with a concentrated intensity. I looked around and was sure that some of the younger professionals were holding their breath. Even the one or two artists that had made it through the huge iron doors of the Jerusalem mansion forgot their diffidence and their artistic rebellion and watched the man in awe.

Rivkah and Rebecca sat across from me at the far end of the table. We were the only children allowed. Them, since the two girls were part of the family consort, and me because my father was probably the most important satellite in Simeon's universe of power.

He began to speak, solemnly, coolly, with something hidden within him. I watched him entranced, not because his words were interesting, and not because he, as a figure, was interesting, but because to me it seemed as if he was snatching emotions and ideas one by one from each of his daughters and speaking them into the air. My father sat next to him, also watching, also thinking his own thoughts. Next to my father sat my mother, resistant, reluctant, anchored by her modesty. And across from my father, to Simeon's right, sat their mother, Sara Simeon, glowing.

Out of the corner of my eye I saw some movement between the twins and immediately sensed one of their conspiracies. Their smiles were tiny, but the glint in their eyes showed me that something was happening. Simeon continued with his speech, which was simple but weighty. He spoke about the Land of Israel, of the people who fill it, of the struggles and the inner essence of the nation. He paused frequently, maybe for effect, maybe to call the words that he meant to his mouth.

During one of the pauses I felt the toe of a shoe touch my shin. It was a tiny little jab, as if done by accident. If anyone aside from Rivkah and Rebecca, or just one of them alone, had been sitting across from me I would have thought it actually had been an accident. But I knew better. I tensed up, waiting. I had only one thing on my mind, one thing so heavy, so serious that I considered praying for it as I sat there: I could not interrupt the speech. I could not be the one to move, to rustle, or, God forbid, to make a noise, a sound, speak a word. The look from my father that I would receive, that I'd received only diluted versions of in the past, would have been thunderous. The bolt of lightning from his eyes, the disapproval that bordered on disavowal, would have cracked me in half. And then my father, after treating me affectionately and lightly for the remainder of the dinner, even allowing me a sip of wine or some other unheard-of privilege that I received only during the Great Shabbos dinners, would have taken the two halves of me home and slowly ground me to dust. This, I could count on.

My heart skipped a beat when the corner of Rebecca's mouth parted in her devilish smile. If Rebecca intended it, it would happen. If it would happen, it would be murderous, deadly. And then it happened: a sharp kick to the shin from Rivkah's pointed shoe. The girl braced herself with both hands on the seat to deliver it. It felt like the shoe was rimmed with a steel spike that happened to land in the one secret bundle of nerves in my shin I never knew I had. I felt queasy for a moment. But I managed to swallow the grunt that jumped from my stomach and tried to escape from my mouth. I kept calm. I allowed my leg to throb. It was okay, my father was sitting at the other end of the table listening, relaxed, uninfuriated.

But then she did it again, the little bitch. I pressed my lips together and glared at her. The look on her face was of contented disinterest. She looked as if she'd kicked the furniture, or kicked nothing at all. By this point I knew the danger was serious — since Rebecca had yet to get directly involved. Doubtless, the plan was hers. And, doubtless, she was using it in part to soothe her sister's anger, her hurt, from the audacious insult she'd dealt her earlier. I tried to stay calm. My face was flushed. I thought for a second of getting up from the table, as if I had to use the bathroom or didn't feel well. But without a medical emergency I would be better off letting my legs get kicked to pulp than stand up from the laid table of the Great Shabbos dinner at the Simeon household.

The blow from Rebecca was vicious. For a second I could feel nothing — in part because the kick was so hard that there was a moment of numbness before the pain, and in part because I was too consumed by the notion of her viciousness, of the bizarre conflagration that burned inside of her. But then the pain came. Tears rolled down my cheeks. I thought she'd broken my leg, I worried for a second that I'd never run again, never ride my bike again, maybe never walk again. But the pain eased quickly, though I sat there with both legs throbbing, maybe bleeding (a whole other ordeal that I'd have to endure if my mother were to find blood on my pants).

Quietly, I slid the folded white napkin from the table and pressed it onto my lap. With one hand resting politely on the table, I used my other hand to unfold the cloth. I then quickly, silently pressed the napkin to my face to dry the tears of pain, dropped the napkin onto my lap, and then looked to the head of the table. Whatever the condition of my legs, if I was now to be wheelchair-bound for the rest of my long life, I was relieved: Simeon was still talking, gently, deeply, and my father was still listening, and it all was going on as if in some other, parallel universe that operated according to its own private logic.

I looked over at the twins and saw them laughing. They weren't laughing out loud, and they were barely just smiling, but their small shoulders were shaking in almost imperceptible spasms and their mouths were curled into shapes of suppressed smiles and one of them put a hand to her nose, as if to cover her mouth. And I was mortified, not because they were laughing at me, at a pain they had just caused me for no reason, but because they were risking the danger that I'd just escaped. One word, one look, one flutter of distraction from Simeon in the direction of the girls, and my fate would be resealed and there would be no reason for me to fast on Yom Kippur.

But we made it through and Simeon thanked his wife for the arrangement of the dinner and sank into his seat and the dinner began. The girls chattered on without mentioning the kicks, without smiling or laughing as they did before. I sat there sulking, insulted, feeling like I'd been ostracized from our society, as if an injustice had been committed. But by the time the main course was being served I returned, in my mind, to the comedy-tragedy of

Rebecca floating down the stairs dressed to make her sister look like a clown. And I thought of the emotion coursing through her twin, the emotion that, for those moments, Rebecca owned. And I could only admire Rebecca for the mastery of our little universe and pity Rivkah for what she didn't have.

Course after course made its way to the table. We were served what the others were served. I looked at some of the food — the caviar, the stuffed trout, the slivers of raw ginger, the poached avocados, as if they were bizarre new life forms found in a tide pool. But Rivkah and Rebecca, without a moment of hesitation, without looking at any bit of the food, picked up the correct fork and knife from the set of silver placed in front of them and ate with their legs gently swinging under the table. When one of them wanted more water, she would move her glass an inch toward the table's edge and one of the servants would fill it quickly.

After dessert small prayer books were passed around. Simeon, with his small black knit kippah, told the guests the page number of the Birkat Hamazon. We made our way through the light maze of benching. Even the young artists, so astute in their resistance to their religion, found themselves mouthing the words they'd been taught as children. Simeon would turn an eye toward one of them and he or she, without knowing why, would start to sing more loudly. Rivkah and Rebecca sat in front of me, singing the prayers and inserting little rephrasings and harmonies into the prayers as they did at school. We finished the prayers; the young artists looked relieved but enlivened. Simeon stood and suggested that the group move into the huge living room where they could sit and talk and drink some coffee.

The girls' mother leaned over to my mother and conferred on something. She, Sara Simeon, then walked toward us as we sat waiting to be excused. She glimmered in her walk, with her silk shawl and the blond hair that refused to explain how the girls were given pale faces and pitch-black bands of hair. She sat down next to Rivkah and placed her forearms across the cleared table so she could whisper to us. The girls, so placid and patient in their child roles during the dinner, turned to their mother with a restrained ecstasy. Rivkah instinctively wrapped her hands around her mother's upper arm and let them hang there as her mother spoke, just to be connected. And even Rebecca turned fully in her seat, sat bolt upright and alternately squeezed each of her fingers in the fist of the other hand, to dispel some of the energy, and pressed her leg to Rivkah's white-stockinged calf, so she could be connected to her mother, through her sister.

"Hi my babies," she said to them. And she leaned over and kissed Rivkah on the cheek and pulled Rebecca to her and kissed her on the forehead. She said hello to me as well and told me I looked handsome and I, calling her "Sara," said thank-you.

"You know who sat at this table, right?" We waited to hear. "All sorts of important people, people from other countries, dignitaries, businessmen, famous writers, a sculptor, Mr. Lipscisz from the orchestra, and your fathers. And all during the dinner, I caught people leaning over and whispering to each other about those three amazing children at the end of the table."

We all smiled as she went on. "Once or twice, when Professor Markowitz said to the man sitting next to her how well behaved the children at the end of the table were, I had to interrupt." We were stunned to hear that Sara would do something as forbidden as interrupt. "I said to her, 'No, Jane, they're not well behaved at all. To say that they're well behaved implies that they're restraining themselves for our sake, that they're trained to act like that. But they're not well behaved children at all — they're adults in miniature, which is why they're sitting at the table with us. Rivkah is a painter and she's made leaps and bounds over the last year. Rebecca is a dancer, but she's flirting with the idea of a change of profession, maybe to academia, like you. And the young man over there in the beautiful dark suit and pale blue tie is a thinker, a writer. They're all very serious people.'"

The three of us laughed quietly at the last statement and Sara smiled and looked at all of us.

"So tell me ladies and gentleman, how did you find the dinner?" she said, affecting a mock-British accent.

"It was perfect Mummy," said Rivkah putting on the same faux British air to continue the joke. "Smashing, darling, really."

"The fish was undercooked," Rebecca smiled.

"Oh was it?" Sara replied, raising an inquisitive eyebrow. Rebecca giggled and caved under the pressure of her mother's question and shook her head.

"And the writer…what will the reviews be like?"

Rivkah and Rebecca looked up, waiting to see how I'd interact with the most important being in their world. Their waiting stares consumed me and for a small second I wasn't sure I'd be able to answer at all. But then I glanced at Rebecca and saw her sitting there with one eyebrow raised slightly, and the look on her face hopeful and forgiving, and it seemed like I could smell the perfume of soap on her body.

"The review will say..." and I paused to pull something to say out of the air, "that if all Israel ate this well there wouldn't be another shot fired in Jerusalem."

The girls looked at Sara, who sat there leaning toward us with a huge smile on her face. She leaned forward and took my chin in her hand and gave my cheeks a squeeze and reminded me that I was a boy. I blushed. The girls were delighted that I'd given their mother the right answer, the answer that made her happy, and they both looked at me with glowing, appreciative faces.

"I have to go back and make sure Aba doesn't get carried away with his politics. But I wanted to tell you that there's something special for you three in the side garden. Shabbat Shalom, you beautiful girls — and boy." We all said Shabbat Shalom and walked quickly into the huge kitchen. Rivkah stopped along the way to sneak into the pantry, step up on her tiptoes and grab a lollipop from one of the high shelves, and then ran after us outside.

The main pathway of the garden was lit with tea lights. We followed them around the first bend of flowers where the tea lights led to large torches stuck into the ground. A few feet from the torches bedouin blankets were laid on the ground and above them silk canopies were hanging open to invite us in. We crept into the tent and looked around at the dozens of colors of the patchwork blankets. Little lights were strung up around the tent. In the middle, on the floor, was a silver tray with tea and cookies waiting for us. Three packages sat on the table next to it.

Rebecca moved to grab a package but Rivkah caught her hand and said, "Let's have tea and then open them." Rebecca, who, I could see, was tempted to respond with a rejection or jibe, checked her impulse as she absorbed the logic of the idea. She sat down without a word and Rivkah poured out the Arab tea. Rebecca raised her handleless teacup and then we raised ours.

"A toast," she said, "to my sister Rivkah."

Rivkah, disbelieving, looked confused. But when she saw Rebecca still holding the cup up in the air, and then saw me waiting for her reaction, she lifted her cup. I repeated the toast — "To Rivkah" — and we clinked cups and sipped the tea, which had been pre-sweetened for us.

"Okay, open them," she said.

We opened our packages. We were all instantly lost in our own little treasures. Mine showed me a perfectly smooth, perfectly white piece of marble with a seal carved into its center. The seal showed a male figure holding a sword in one hand and a plate in the other. Inside the package there was a note that said, "Jerusalem. Babylonian Period Seal."

The girls opened their presents — a small gem for each of them. I didn't know what they were, but they were beautiful. They looked at the stones, held them out in their hands, held them to their foreheads, giddy, lost in their excitement. Playing with their new presents, showing them off to each other, they looked like the same person, the same girl trying on a new piece of jewelry in a mirror that slightly distorted the hue of the gem. I laughed to myself, amused that they were so enraptured by the presents, knowing that by the next day they wouldn't even remember that they'd been given a gift.

We sat in our bedouin tent and I listened to the girls talk about their classmates and friends. They spoke about some of their clothes and other important things. They asked me if I enjoyed dinner. I glared at them and then rolled my pant legs and showed them the purple, black and blue bruises blooming on my shins. Rivkah paused and looked at my legs. She seemed to be lost in the pattern of the bruises. Her hand raised itself off the ground and looked as if it was going to caress my bruised leg. But Rebecca shifted slightly and Rivkah, awoken from her trance of remorse, picked a thread off my pant leg, put her hand on the ground and rested her head on her shoulder. I looked at Rivkah, at her face, and then Rivkah looked up at me for a moment. We might have forgotten ourselves for a second, maybe we would have touched, acted as if there weren't a third body there, an interlocutor. But Rebecca grunted out a laugh as she watched us, and then she was suppressing giggles, and then she was laughing full-throated, with hand and arm curled around her belly. She plopped over on the floor, to taunt us, to laugh harder, to remind us who we were. Rivkah tried for a second to smile and then tried to turn the smile into a laugh, so she could return to her sister. But she couldn't, and the effort, which I saw, twisted her face into an embarrassing jumble. She turned to Rebecca and said, "What the hell is so funny? Stop laughing — you're annoying me. Stop. Shut up." Rebecca laughed harder and Rivkah got angrier. She hit her sister on the leg and Rebecca calmed down for a second and sat up. She gave us a few seconds and then started to laugh again. I got up and went inside. Rivkah also got up and left the tent, but went somewhere else, probably some place in the garden she knew of.

In the kitchen, the staff was washing the dishes and bringing out cups of coffee and tea and carts of desserts. Sara walked into the kitchen and saw me.

"What's going on, Aaron?" she asked.

I shrugged and smiled.

"Those girls being cruel to you?"

I smiled again, "No, Rebecca's just joking around. You know."

Sara smiled. "Well, come with me. There's a conversation you'll be interested in."

We went into the great, high-ceilinged living room together. Rivkah was already there, leaning against her father's chair, gently playing with a small flower that she'd stuck into his buttonhole. I looked around for Rebecca, but she wasn't there. I listened to the guests having their literary and artistic conversations. It seemed as if most of them, at least those who spoke, were fulfilling an obligation by speaking — as if they were speaking so they could check a box next to their name before they left.

Simeon sat on his chair, arms on the armrests, listening, looking around. Sara guided the conversation to the places she wanted it to be — to what she called her "pet projects" which, in truth, were her alternating obsessions. At one point, she was dedicated to finding drinking-water solutions for Africans. Later (or maybe before), she became interested in preserving old prayer books. Then she started to study Kabbalah and then she started to edge toward politics. One thing that distinguished her from other professional (or, in other words, wealthy) dilettantes was that she never forgot about previous obsessions. She continued to write articles for environmental magazines, discussing advances in desalination research. She went to her Kabbalah studies regularly, and she still poured money into the organizations she knew of that salvaged old sidurim from destruction.

She managed to find responses and seed ideas

in the conversations that, after two or three rounds of back-and-forth, the obligatory comments from Professor Markowitz (and the snivel of dissent from her rival, Dassah Levi, the playwright), would lead the whole group just to where she wanted them. No one was ever bored and everyone who spoke, and sometimes even those who didn't, felt that their opinions had been considered and that they'd had some sway on Mr. and Mrs. Simeon, and they all drove home propped up with pride.

Simeon looked down at his daughter who stood next to him, resting her head on his chest.

"Where is your sister, my baby?"

She hummed the sound of "I don't know" without opening her mouth.

"Maybe we should go find her," he said, meaning, "Go get her."

She raised her head up and looked at him. Then she looked at me with her tired eyes, with an expression of being stung twice during the night, asking with her eyes for me to save her another humiliation. I spoke up. "I'll go find her," and left the room as Rivkah put her head against her father's chest again.

I half expected to return to the tent and find

Rebecca still laughing. I thought I'd scare her or play some trick on her. I crept up to the tent silently, crouching a little, ready to jump and scream "boo!" I folded back the first flap and stopped instantly. Instead of seeing the girl I expected — laughing, playing with her sister's gift as well as her own — I came across Rebecca lying on her side with her knees drawn halfway to her chest. Her hair was spread out underneath her and one arm lay on the ground and the other rested softly on her side. Her eyes were staring off into nothing. She, for a few seconds, didn't move, didn't look away from whatever she was dreaming about. And then, without any particular reason, she looked at me, into my eyes. She froze me there for a second or two, staring, wondering. Slowly, a smile spread across her face. Not the cruel, taunting smile, but a plaintive one, an innocent one.

She lifted herself up and rested on one hand. And then she got up and followed me back into the house.

The guests filed out of the house soon after. Some of them, the religious and those who lived close by, set out to walk back home. Others started up Mercedes and BMWs, and the headlights of the big cars poured over the mist and fog of the cool

Jerusalem night. Rivkah and Rebecca sleepily walked upstairs without saying goodbye to the guests. Rivkah, as she put her foot on the second stair of the staircase, managed to mumble, "See you, Aaron." Rebecca didn't say anything at all.

$\approx$

In and out of their lives, always there but never there, because they always disappeared behind a veil of privacy, of family. They went home and I imagined they went to live in the revived ruins of some sunken city. Nothing would have surprised me about their home life, in the lofty mansion of Jerusalem or high-rise apartment in Tel Aviv. I thought that I too went to my home, to my private world. But my private world was routine and regulated. It was the light scraping of knives and forks against plates in a context of silence. It was my mother mumbling to my father that something needed to be done, and my father mumbling an assent.

My parents' house was light, even lovely. When a visitor walked in they saw open space and light. They saw my mother's taste, an intelligent taste that found art in engineering schematics, in framed pages of old texts, in rare species of flowers, in the perfect shape of the windows. They saw my father's solidity, the marks of his dominion, the lines of books in various rooms, polished pipes he never smoked, translations of the Bible in three languages laid open on tables, a plate of cheese and fruit cut by a silver knife.

My father would smile lightly when he saw his name in an obscure journal for bibliophiles, mentioning a rare edition he managed to find. "It's not just the knowledge," he'd say, probably echoing a saying of his father's, which in turn was probably something Talmudic. "It's the knowledge of the knowledge."

My mother would huff at his little sayings. She found them extravagant and, in a way, indecent. She'd turn muttering and go look for something that needed cleaning or, if she was in a harder mood, she'd sit down and continue writing an article she wanted to finish. My father would laugh to himself and then look at me and laugh more. He'd turn away, laughing, quietly and then expansively, until he got to his study, where he would shut the door.

A visitor would walk into the house and see my father extending his padded hand to them and laughing with his eyes. They see my mother gathering a bunch of flowers together and putting them into a vase, as if for them. They see the quiet Shabbat table, laid already on Thursday evening, waiting for us, more patient than the sea. They see bowls of unrecognizable fruit glowing in purple and fuchsia hues next to ordinary red apples and engorged oranges.

I looked around that house and saw only a gray mist. There was no darkness, no tales of horror or abuse or neglect. There was a gray mist that shrouded all their colorful intellectual toys. There was the gray mist that was them and their lives — their need to live in movement, in constant mental motion that caused them to hang art and books on the walls in order to have something permanent of themselves. They took their ideas and froze them in objects and the gradual accumulation of objects came to stand for the people.

My mother's love was buried deep inside her. The pressure of her great, compressed personality had made her love — for me, for my father, maybe even for the world — into a diamond that lay buried in her core. The sharp edges of that stone needled her. It was like every emotional event, every movement of emotion, jarred the stone which cut and lacerated her insides, causing her to make a great effort to stay as still as possible.

My father lived oppositely. Instantly, he brought

everything out, so it wouldn't have to be inside. In spite of all the clutter of his erudite hobbies, he had no passion for anything. I, his son, seemed to be one of his intellectual playthings. Behind his study door is where I imagined his real life to be. What it was, what he did in it, I had no idea. But if someone had told me he had been writing a true history of the universe or an anatomy of God, it wouldn't have surprised me.

They managed to get along. They built their house efficiently like two worker bees servicing a greater unknown. The house grew. They put a small greenhouse in the yard. They added rooms and libraries, they hung portraits and works of art. They were fulfilling a plan that had been laid for them generations in advance, in decrepit sitting-rooms of Europe, by Jews who cut their candles in half and swept the crumbs of the challah into a dish so they could be used with next week's meat.

I never hated them. In fact I admired them, maybe even loved them. I looked at my father the way a young man looks at a heroic statue. When the sculpture looked down from the pedestal and spoke to me I listened, I heard every single one of the words, I thought for days on end about their meaning, and in the end, I threw them in the garbage. What could a statue tell me? It was only his favorite remark about falling off the camel that meant something to me.

My mother rarely spoke. She said plenty of words, giving instructions to this person, directions to that person, corrections to the other one. She spoke calmly, meticulously, to the maid about how to clean the corners properly, and she gave lectures to the cook about the cholent. My guess is that if anyone had ever listened to her, they would have found her to be completely right about whatever it was she was saying. The problem is she said nothing worth hearing.

Only in her most agitated states — a force of feeling that would have burst into rage in someone with slightly less control than her — when she sat down at her writing table and unleashed herself on the pen and pad, was there a human voice flowing from her body.

I look back at some of her articles and books and I'm shocked to think the author of those works was my mother, the person I knew and experienced every day. Her written words were as crystalline as her living attitude, but the passion in their meaning was wild, sometimes even radical. She left dozens, if not hundreds of essays to the world, and a small handful of books. Deep in her clothes drawer I later found a small book of poetry she wrote, probably the only copy ever printed.

My father's work was known in his lifetime, but his approach to it was different. He was haughty, his writing laughed at its reader. He was always laughing, and guests in our house — walking along the pine floor, running their hands along the Turkish tapestries covering Jerusalem stone, looking at the pink insides of conch shells on dark wood tables — found something light about him, as if he were jester to a philosopher king.

But he wasn't. My father was a lawyer. He was a brilliant lawyer with brilliant tastes and brilliant opinions. Some have called him one of the country's greatest legal minds, but I doubt that's true. But he lived in the law, he wore it on his back, and saw the world through its structure.

This was the honeycomb I lived in; but to the bee, the honey isn't so sweet. Rivkah and Rebecca were. They were something else, they were real life, freedom. I don't know what I was to them. Maybe I could have guessed what I meant to each of them as individuals, but to them two together, and to the shared ideas that superseded their individual thoughts, I could never know.

The three of us grew together. It's amazing, looking back on it, that there was no interruption. That for so many years we never let anyone else in, never cared that there were people outside our world, that there were other kids at our school, who did things together. But things started to change. Our bodies were the first thing. Them before me. They became taller, there were curves, there were hidden suggestions of things I didn't know about. And then me, after them. It was the feeling of the change that I noticed most. And, of course, it was the feeling in relation to them. They weren't just Rivkah and Rebecca anymore. They were more than that. In my eyes they seemed to disassemble into parts.

I saw this one day while we were sitting around in their backyard, doing nothing. Rivkah with a magazine, Rebecca curled up on a garden chair, either sleeping or pretending to be asleep. I sat on the grass doing nothing. I looked up and saw Rivkah turn the page of her magazine. But I wasn't looking at Rivkah. I was looking at her arms. They were so white. They almost stung my eyes. I didn't understand what it was, why they looked like something I wanted to have, like something I wanted to consume. And then I looked at the girl herself and saw her sitting there absorbed in her magazine and I wanted her to stay exactly like that, forever, to be sitting there with thin legs drawn up, ankles bare, feet rubbing against each other in a slow rhythm, the rest of the world gone, a passive, almost stupid, look on her face. But at the same time I felt that I wanted to jump up and pull her off the chair and take her somewhere else where I could make her into something I owned.

I blinked and turned my head and saw Rebecca curled up, her head turned sideways and resting on the back of the chair, her eyes open and staring at me. She was watching me watch her sister. She saw me see something new. She didn't move. Rivkah turned a page and then dropped the magazine and got up to go inside, clutching the side of her long skirt as she walked barefoot. For the first time, maybe ever, I was able to disregard Rebecca. I looked only at Rivkah walking into the house, each movement so ordinary, so unseen (but yet seen), so like a thing that should be hidden but was walking around in plain view.

Once she disappeared into the house I looked back at Rebecca. She had closed her eyes again and was breathing rhythmically but not heavily.

After that day, something changed. Rebecca kept her distance. She spoke to me and interacted with me, but that's how I knew things were different. She stopped playing her vicious pranks on me, and making barbed comments. She stopped giving me the silent treatment for hours or days at a time without any specific reason why. She spoke to me calmly, cordially, as if she still knew me, but also as if she had made a decision about something.

I took refuge in Rivkah. All the things that Rivkah had always wanted to do — riding our bikes to the stream near the house, going to the German Colony stores together, making homemade tehina or hummus — we did. Rebecca, in these long autumn afternoons, mostly stayed in that garden chair. Sometimes she would go up to her room where she did things that no one knew. Rivkah and I, so used to being the target of her affectionate abuse, felt like we'd won some prolonged war, or that we at least could gloat with each other that we were winning, that we were there, downstairs or outside together, while Rebecca was sullen.

Rivkah and I decided to take our bikes to Ein Kerem one afternoon after school. We got everything ready — water, some fruit, a small picnic blanket — and started our ride. It was shorter than we expected. We got there and rode around the narrow streets, past the stone houses, until we got to the convent. Rivkah knew a secret way onto the grounds, which were filled with stunning gardens and a small forest of brush and swooping trees.

We found a patch of wild grass and laid out the blanket. We shared some *shesek* and melon and drank some water. She told me a joke she heard that day. It wasn't funny, but I laughed. I watched her take a bite of shesek, and again I was frozen. She held the fruit with her fingertips and stared down at it as she chewed. She took another piece of fruit and handed it to me without asking if I wanted it or not. I took it, but I could only look at her face, her lips. I could only feel the freedom of Rebecca's absence. And this time, consciously, I looked at her thin arms, and looked back at her face, and then looked down to her neck, her collarbone, the slope of skin delineated by her shirt.

She looked up at me and said, "What are you doing?"

It took me a few moments to understand what she had said, and even then I didn't know why she'd said it. I looked at her, eyes the color of near-frozen water, and saw her look down at my hand, which I saw was holding her forearm.

"I don't know," I said, but I left my hand there. She stopped chewing. She looked at me calmly, patiently. It was as if she understood this as an event, as something that she'd been expecting and had now arrived. She planted her hand on the blanket and shifted towards me. Her legs were bent away from me, two overlapping V's. Her free hand resting on one thigh. She looked at me without flinching. We both had some nervousness, not about the situation, but that somewhere Rebecca might be lurking, might be waiting to jump out of a bush and fall into hysterical laughter, pointing at us, mocking us into shame. But she wasn't there.

Rivkah leaned toward me more and then pressed her lips against mine. I tasted the shesek mixed with the strange texture and taste of skin. She put her free hand through my hair. I ran my hand from her forearm up to her shoulder. I don't know how long we stayed there but it felt like it could, or should, have been forever. But the next thing I knew, we were lying on the blanket, she on her side, me on my back, head turned to face her, staring and smiling at each other. It was as if a new world had been discovered. We could be patient now since we knew our discovery was waiting for us, and that it was safe from other people's hands. My heart was full but, somehow, heavy. I was happier than I'd ever been but felt a tiny pinhole of doubt, a little rend in the perfectness of this girl with black hair and riverflowing eyes — the feeling, much, much less than a thought, that I had sinned.

We avoided Rebecca entirely in the following days and weeks, and Rebecca avoided the world. Rivkah and I thought she was doing it deliberately, to demonstrate to us that she didn't care, that she wasn't concerned about what we, the inferior, might be doing with our time. But we never spoke about it. It's unlikely that in those few weeks we even mentioned her name once.

The days were mostly like that first day — wandering around together, sometimes falling into a kiss, sometimes more than a kiss. At some point we felt like grown-up lovers, going to the shops together, making plans for the next day, pretending to be much more busy than we actually were. It was Rivkah's game, a game she passionately loved, and I played along with it.

I enjoyed it but felt at each step I was looking back. I was wondering what was happening. I would fall asleep at night, after the first few days of the romance, thinking not about Rebecca but about my parents, thinking what they might say to me if they found out, thinking that I might have shamed them, or thinking that I might have shamed myself, in front of God. And then I'd think about Rivkah, lying in her own bed at night, thinking about me while I was not thinking about her. And on top of the guilt I felt for betraying my parents, for offending God, I felt the guilt of disappointing her in thought. I slept less and less, each time crawling into bed with some sense of dread, some drastic desire for it to be morning so I could run back to Rivkah, to see her, to give her our morning peck on the lips, to sneak away to the fields behind the train station, to sit in a cafe together (like the other couples of the city) or, once in a while, to sneak up to her bedroom when no one was looking.

It was there one day that we heard it. It was a sound we hadn't heard. Some kind of hacking, choking. We looked at each other — Rivkah lying across her bed, me sitting on the floor with my back against the side of the bed. We both had the same initial thought: She's back. We froze in fear that some new onslaught was about to begin. That all this time of quiet, Rebecca was hatching new plans, fortifying, rearming. We waited listening. We went back to doing nothing. But after a few minutes we heard it again. That hacking and choking. But this time it wasn't stopping. Rivkah looked at me and said "Aaron," as if she wanted to know what we should do.

I started to get up, but before I was standing Rivkah had jumped up and was walking toward the door. I followed her out of her room and into the hallway that connected her room with her sister's. Rebecca's door was closed and in any other case her sister would never have dared to enter the room without asking. But with the choking sounds coming from behind the door she grabbed the handle to open the door. I put my hand on her elbow, unsure why, maybe to stop her, to warn her, but she didn't look at me. She opened the door and walked into the room.

Neither Rivkah nor I will ever forget what we saw there. Neither of us will forget the ramifications of the sight, the events that tumbled after it with greater momentum, greater efficiency, as the days flew by. The bigness of our first kiss, between Rivkah and me, was annihilated. I couldn't help thinking that Rebecca had once again managed to trump her sister. But this time, Rivkah had no such thought or feeling.

Rebecca was in the middle of her room. The room was its usual mess, clean (since the maids dusted and vacuumed every day) but strewn with clothes, books, tawny jewelry, gifts. The blinds were closed but there was enough light to see. And even without seeing, it was enough to hear.

She was on her hands and knees. She was coughing and hacking like she was trying to bring up something stuck deep inside her. But it was already coming up — blood and mucus mixed together. A small pool of it had already stained the carpet. The girl was bent over coughing like this, without intention or understanding of what was happening. It was as if she stopped existing as a person for those moments and was only a sick thing coughing.

Rivkah screamed and ran to her. She fell to her knees and grabbed Rebecca's arm. She started saying my name over and over, "Aaron, Aaron, Aaron." I didn't know what to do. I started to turn to get help but as I did Sara Simeon rushed through the door, having heard one of her daughters scream, and gasped when she saw Rebecca spitting out blood. The rest of that day is black; I remember nothing.

That blackness seemed to stay in the house and grow, as if it were alive. There seemed to be less light coming in through the vaulted windows (and with the approach of winter, maybe there was). Black rings grew underneath Sara Simeon's eyes. An occasional glimpse of Simeon himself showed a man who had fallen into shadow.

The blackness was the reflection of an absence — the absence of Rebecca. She was there, somewhere, behind the door to her room. I didn't understand at the time what it was inside her lungs that had made her cough blood and spew a subtle, insidious blackness into the lives of the Simeons — and into my own life as well. Strangely (thinking about it now), I never returned to the question, never asked my father or mother, never asked anyone else, the name they were all murmuring during those days, the strange medical word that sounded grotesque to me because its syllables were playful, changed timbre twice through the word, but were held together by a meaning of illness.

There was only one spot of light in the night sky of the Simeon household: Rivkah. Rivkah continued to wear her bright pastel dresses. She continued to put teardrop earrings in her ears. She continued to pick strange little flowers from the garden. At first I was a little shocked by it. I thought her sensitivity was sharper than that, that it would have affected her more than anyone else. Gradually I realized that initial thought was true. To everyone else, Rebecca's suffering was a point of blackness in the light of life, something to be drawn into, a radiating black mass. But for Rivkah it was the opposite — it was a searing sun, a misery so intense that it would burn her.

She never gave in to it. She continued, acting as if her twin, the only person who ever lived and ever would live to be exactly like her, the only person who knew her secretly and instinctively, had something like a bad cold and would soon get better. I imagine now that it might have occurred to her that if her twin, her exact likeness, were to die she would ipso facto die as well. And maybe for this she approached Rebecca with light. That she brought her coughing sister trays of tea sweetened with honey and decorated with little hand-painted porcelain vases bearing the tiniest and most exquisite flowers she could find.

For the first few weeks after Rebecca's return from the hospital I watched as Rivkah would knock gently on her sister's door and, with a smile on her face, enter the room. She would close the door most of the way but always leave it a little open, as if to make sure that the light of the outside world was still there for her to pull herself back into life.

Rivkah came out of the room each time empty. The tray of tea or cookies or flowers or schoolwork was gone, out of her hands. The smile was gone with it. And while she tried to keep her back straight and her head up, and as she inhaled each time, as if to keep herself propped up — to keep herself alive — I saw through all these little gestures and efforts of self-preservation as if they were glass.

But still she and I would walk to the valleys of Ein Kerem, or we would sit in the cafes and sweeten our coffee, or we would pick fruit from wild fruit trees. And all of it was dust. Only in the moments of extreme need, when Rebecca's sickness had finally managed to worm its way into Rivkah's heart, would she feel me as a real person. During these moments the world around her dissolved — as it had for everyone else. The cafe would fade into charcoal, the fruit trees would instantly drop all their fruits, wither, and disappear, the fall sky get covered with the cloud of sadness, and nothing would ever remain. Except me. And while in all those moments before the illness Rivkah pretended to be with me as longtime lovers are with each other, these times of her sadness actually brought her to me. She would lean against me, this girl barely a teenager, and she would turn her head up and look at me for a second, as if to make sure I was still there. And she would sigh out some of the darkness that everyone else was breathing.

It could have been only Sara Simeon to bring me to her daughter — the other one. I don't know if in the first few weeks Rivkah ever thought of bringing me into that room. If she did, it's not something she ever would have actually suggested. It wasn't jealousy or fear that kept her from asking me to come see Rebecca, or from even making a small gesture with her hand or head as she opened the door. It was simply the single-mindedness. Rivkah knew only one thing during those days: making her sister better.

Sara Simeon knew more things. She watched once as Rivkah took some new magazines she'd bought for Rebecca, opened the door, went into the room, and closed the door most of the way, but not all the way. Sara Simeon was standing near the top of the stairs. She looked like a statue of grief that had once been human. She clutched a dark shawl around her shoulders. Her face looked worn — not exactly tired, but as if a constant flow of tears had polished her skin into raw stone. I looked back at her and tried to smile, thinking back to the Great Shabbos dinner when she'd complimented me so graciously.

The smile woke her from her trance. She smiled back at me, sympathetically. "Why don't you go in there and say hello?" she said.

I looked at her for a minute. I didn't know what to do, or what not to do, or why not to do it. I felt there was a possibility that to do so would be somehow rude — that the door to Rebecca's room wasn't a door but a rule.

"It's okay. I know she wants to see you. And you must want to see her too. Tell her I'll be in to say hello in a few minutes."

I told her okay and walked toward the door. I pushed it open. I didn't know what I was doing. I didn't know what ghost of Rebecca lay in that bed. I stepped into the room and saw two pairs of the same eyes look over at me. Rivkah was standing to the side of the bed. She turned and looked at me over her shoulder, smiling her smile. Rebecca looked at me too.

What shocked me was that it was Rebecca — not some approximation of Rebecca, not a corpse of Rebecca, or a ghost of her. She was thin and pale. The room was darker than it usually was but it wasn't the bizarre crypt I secretly feared. Rebecca had a board propped up on a pillow that sat on her lap. On the board was a picture she was drawing with colored pencils. Rivkah was looking at it, fascinated by her sister's ability.

"So where have you been? Are you afraid of me?" she asked, bulging her eyes out of her head mockingly.

I didn't know what to say. "No, I —"

"I know," she said, wheezing a little. "Just don't expect me to come visit you when I'm better and you're sick." She paused here for effect. Then she smiled. I smiled too.

"Shut up you idiot," I shot back at her.

"Ooh, really witty Aaron." I had nothing to say about that.

"How do you feel?"

"Oh, yeah. I feel great," she said sarcastically.

"Though at least I don't have to go to school. Those idiots there make me want to shoot myself." Rivkah, I could see, had the urge to remind Rebecca that she actually liked school, that she had a lot of friends, and everyone missed her. She held herself back for a moment but eventually gave in to herself.

"But Rebs," she said, looking not at her sister's eyes but at the bedspread, "you like school. And we've had a substitute for the last week. He's a total idiot but it's funny to watch him. You'll love it."

Rebecca looked like a stunned animal. She couldn't understand what she was supposed to do — grab her sister's hand and hold it or shoot back some venomous comment and make the sister blush. She looked at me. I wanted to help her, to say something to Rivkah to diffuse the tension inside Rebecca. But I couldn't. I looked at Rebecca's face as she looked at me. She was a helpless thing. A single strand of hair was caught in the corner of her mouth. Her crystal blue eyes were slightly red around the edges. Her skin showed the first signs of imperfection it ever had. She lay in a bed while her twin stood above her.

It was the first time I ever saw Rebecca. All the other times had been clouded by Rivkah, by their secret wars, and by Rebecca herself. It was the first time Rebecca was the one looking at me, the one asking me for something, for help, for an answer.

"Well anyways," a voice said, "you'll be back soon whether you like it or not." It was Rivkah. Her need to inject a dose of positivity at every possible point broke the impasse and Rebecca looked down at her legs covered by the blankets. She looked exhausted.

"I'm going to go see what's for lunch. If it's tuna, I'll find the person responsible. Do you want anything?"

Rebecca shook her head. Rivkah smiled, touched her sister's hand, and rushed out of the room. She shut the door behind her.

There was a silence for a second or two that threatened to grow into something huge and uncontrollable. I didn't know what to say — to apologize, to lamely ask again how she felt, to make some sort of comment — and she, lying there and staring at her legs as if they were once things that were involved in her life but no longer were, also kept quiet. I was about to mumble something about going to see if Rivkah needed help (help with what I hadn't thought about) when Rebecca looked up at me.

"So." She said it and smiled. Her eyes narrowed fiercely as if the thought of herself — her real self, her unsick self — had just occurred to her.

"So?" I asked, trying to sound innocent, already sensing what her single-word sentence meant but hopeful that I could diffuse it by playing dumb.

"So how has it been between you and Captain Happy?"

"What do you mean?"

"What do you mean," she repeated after me in a retard's voice. "You know what I mean. You two are running up and down all of Jerusalem with your mouths clamped together. So...is she a good kisser?"

I opened my mouth to give some kind of answer (though I wasn't sure what), when Rebecca interrupted. "Do you love her? Are you planning a family? Did she have an abortion?" She was smiling like the devil. It looked like this was the first time she'd been happy since being cloistered in her bedroom.

"Very funny," I said dryly.

"I don't think so. I think it's pretty serious. Little Rivkie, little Rivkaleh," she said, repeating the pet names Simeon used for Rivkah (but conveniently forgetting the ones he had for her). "She's growing up so fast. Soon my father will buy your father a car for you and you can stuff Rivkie in the back seat and get *aaamorous* with her."

This infuriated me — as it was designed to. I was looking down at the same bedspread Rebecca had been looking at and thought of the perfect response — one so simple and so sharp that it would cut her in half. I lifted my head so I could look her in the eye to say it. But then I saw her there. It wasn't viciousness on her face. It wasn't jealousy or anger. It was joy — she was happy. Tiny little creases formed at the corners of her mouth as she smiled and I realized that as much as I'd seen the same creases on the corners of Rivkah's mouth all the times she pretended to smile in the past few weeks, I hadn't seen them on Rebecca's. They were different — they were hers, and for weeks they had been gone.

I did the only thing I could do. I sat down on the bed next to her and smiled. I thought about it — it actually was funny. Get "amorous" with her. I couldn't imagine where she'd picked that up, or how she'd made it up. I looked around the room. A few long strands of colored silk streamed from above the bed to some random place on a wall. Things, for the first time since I'd known Rebecca, were in their place. The room was pretty, unpretentious. There was very little on the walls, unlike Rivkah's room which was decorated down to the millimeter and which changed every week or two as her taste and the trends around her changed.

From here everything was clearer. I'd always known Rivkah as the woundable one. Rivkah as the one streaming into the bathroom with tears running down her face or storming off in humiliation after a casually brutal remark from Rebecca. But Rivkah always came back, sometimes hours, sometimes minutes later, with the tear-water having freshened her up, her mood floating up again toward the sky, ready to be with the people around her. But Rebecca was something else — the opposite or, to be more specific, the complement. Her baseline was melancholy. As she got older the melancholy grew and became more intense. The barbs, the insults, the jokes, the pranks, the haughtiness, it was her attempt to stay away from it, a constant running uphill.

Now she lay in the room sick. She knew what Rivkah and I were up to. Thinking about it stabbed me with sadness and shame. Rebecca sat here all this time — even before she got sick — and we traipsed around kissing, touching each other, drinking coffee. And even while she was sick we were running away from her (and her illness), dressed nicely, looking happy, and she was in the room sick.

She must have seen it on my face. "Listen," she said, "I was just kidding. It's just a joke."

I looked up at her. Her eyes were pleading. She was concerned. I couldn't let her feel worried. I looked at her carefully, looked at her hand, her white arm, her collarbone peeking out of the pajamas, the steep curve of her chin, the earlobe, the strands of hair sweeping down in front of her ears, her slightly red cheeks, her blue eyes, her black hair. It had to be one of it, something. I had to be careful. I had to choose as if my life depended on the choice (and, looking back, it might have). I was filled with a shaking that seemed to start in my stomach and flutter its way up throughout my whole torso and into my arms and hands, which it made cold. There was a pressure in my ears and an anxiety spreading through me.

I saw myself doing it before I was doing it. Then it was actually happening. My hand moving toward her, up toward her head, but then up more specifically to her face, and then my fingertips touched her cheekbones, my palm against her cheek, and gently slid down her cheek and then curved off toward her lips, grazing the bottom one, and lingering there.

Her sister, when I'd grabbed her arm in Ein Kerem, had asked me what I was doing. Rebecca did no such thing. She tilted her head forward and kissed the side of my finger. She looked at me anxiously. There was fear and dread and sadness in her eyes. She turned away from me and put her head on the pillow. She didn't make any sound, she didn't even move, but I thought she was crying.

I don't know how or why I left the room. But when I did it seemed like I had walked into an empty house. Sara Simeon hadn't come in to say hello. Rivkah was somewhere "seeing what's for lunch." Simeon was probably buried inside his study, or maybe at work where the long shadow of his daughter's illness could only just barely reach him.

I walked down the stairs alone. I didn't look for anyone (and they didn't look for me). I opened the big front doors and let myself out. And, for the first time, I left the Simeon household without feeling as if I was abandoning a mystery.

It was always there, when she was sitting in front of the mirror, getting dressed, that I understood her most and understood my life least. Putting on the earrings, then doing the makeup. Touching perfume to the wrists, taking the last look at her hair, and all done with the practiced perfection of a rich girl. There she was, and I was watching her, passing back and forth past the door, getting ready for the big event, putting on my tie, tying my shoes, pretending to be lost in the privacy of my own ritual but always watching.

She was beautiful. Still, the electric sense of amazement of love, still there. And it thrilled me to know her routine as well as I knew her, because that half-conscious process of "getting ready" showed exactly who she was.

Then the diamonds were always last. The necklace, the one I'd bought almost casually, despite the cost, something I thought should be done, and then was done. But for her it was something that existed beyond itself. She liked the diamonds but diamonds she was used to. Gold, silver, platinum, titanium, white gold, tanzanite, amethyst, emerald — used to it. I was wedded to a woman who, in material terms, couldn't be impressed. And she loved the necklace I bought her as if it had been made from a stone so precious it couldn't be bought.

Rivkah, always there, always loving. Putting on the necklace, and loving. In the house, around the city, thinking of the moon, loving. I stood looking at her once again, this time unabashed. She put the necklace on.

Where had we come from? Where were we now? The question hits me, as it often does, and I stand transfixed like an old man searching for the past. But it's always unrecoverable, as if it had returned to the opaque silence of the future, where it belongs.

My attempt to gather it up, to fill my arms with my life, always begins with Rivkah. There she is, those years ago, in uniform, on the bus filled with people looking just like her, and just like me, wearing the same drab olive army uniform. The bus rides were never one thing: On Friday morning, collecting young soldiers from the bases at the end of the week, there was a mutual exhaustion that lay over the passengers like a thick blanket. Some would sit listening to music, dazing at the window, some fast asleep, some typing a series of messages into their phones. At the beginning of the week the rides would begin the same way — sleepy, groggy, grumpy at being disturbed from a two-day flow of toasted breads and cheap cheeses, and sleep. But within an hour, and with every next bus stop filled with soldiers waiting, the bus would wake up, the music get louder, the chatting and talking and flirting begin.

I was on hundreds of those army bus rides. If I were to sit down with a pen and paper, I could probably calculate thousands. I went from the Good Fence down to the Jezreel Valley, through the unreal deserts and spiny ridges of the wadis, to semi-secret army bases, Zionist museums, airfields, and half-developed cities. And I remember only one thing: Rivkah on the bus. This child of superb wealth, who once crawled and toddled in halls of power, with her hair pulled back, her ugly collar open, lightly sweating, holding a big black gun on her lap, looking at me.

We sat next to each other, or in the two aisle seats across from each other. Sometimes I bribed, threatened, and argued in order to change seats so I could sit next to her. But if Rivkah was on that bus, and I was on that bus, we would sit together.

I marveled at her. Every time seeing her as if she was a strange new girl walking onto the bus,

looking like she had come from any little town or
village, from any tile-floored house with crumbling
stucco and a water heater sitting on the roof like an
oversized battery. I never knew what kind of fights,
what insane stubbornness or machinations she
needed to get Simeon to make a phone call on her
behalf — in this case, unlike every other case in the
country, to get the army to draft her, to enlist her,
since there was without doubt a bevy of generals,
attachés, assistant ministers, and faceless functionaries
who each would have thought it their own personal
responsibility to stamp the file of Simeon's daughter
with an exemption, lose a draft order, or make a
quick phone call issuing a command that wouldn't
be questioned.

   She knew this without ever being told. She knew
that if things were left to their direction, she wouldn't
serve, or, at most, would be offered six months in
the most plush and plumb position. She wouldn't
have it. I laughed every time I thought of her or
saw her in front of a group of her soldiers, them
running around in confused circles when she gave
a ridiculously small amount of time to accomplish
a task — always failing to achieve it, even late —
or when she walked behind a line of fighters lying

on their bellies, giving them instruction on how to shoot the rifle, load the mortar, or pull the pin on the grenade.

If once or twice she caught me smirking at her, she, outranking me, would walk up to me screaming, telling me to do push-ups (which I wouldn't do), and then pushing me with a violent jerk of her tiny frame in a direction away from her and the unit she was training. Just at the last second of this seemingly humiliating encounter, I would catch that tiny smile, the half-wink, a little look of treason that told me our own little alliance out-commanded the entire army of Israel. I walked away, keeping up the show, swearing under my breath, kicking dirt, enjoying the laughter and derision of the privates who watched as I was manhandled by their girl sergeant.

On the weekends Rivkah once again became a Simeon. She returned on Friday afternoons to her own Jerusalem apartment, furnished in suede, with thick carpeting cleaned by invisible maids, oversized showerheads, a fridge full of food and a cupboard full of wine. When it had come to setting up the apartment for Rivkah, there wasn't ever much discussion. It was unorthodox and, in a different world, would never have happened. But in this world, in this life, it couldn't have been any other way. Sara Simeon traveled often, leaving the Jerusalem mansion mostly in the hands of the staff. Rivkah and I would come back on a Friday to find postcards from preposterous places — Kyrgyzstan, Liberia, Tucson, Arizona — always addressed to both of us, telling us about some newly discovered collection of abandoned sidurim, about invented techniques for digging desert wells, whatever else. Sometimes packages would arrive, sometimes entire letters. Rivkah would look at each of them carefully, her head turning inside itself, putting the letter or postcard in a proper place of logic to explain why her mother was there, where she was, why we were here on a Friday afternoon alone together, why her great father had become a deep and silent stone.

Rebecca. Never could I — who was not her twin, not her sister or blood — say that name or think it without the pressure of tears coming to my throat, drawing against my eyes. Never could I possess those three syllables without knowing the feeling of a world destroyed, and a new, different one begun and coldheartedly put in its place. This, all the infinite wrongness contained in the cliché that life moves on, was what I felt. And I was not her twin, her sister, or her blood.

I don't know that Rivkah ever said again her sister's name. Maybe one day in the future, far from now, or even tomorrow, that event will occur. But I can't remember it happening, and if it had I would have been shocked, maybe even offended by it.

Rivkah couldn't return to her parents' home all through those army Shabbatot because there was no home to return to. The house still stood there, maybe falling with each particle of dust, but inside it had been dissolved. Sometimes we went to my parents for a Shabbat meal, walking forty-five minutes there and back in a rare Jerusalem snowfall, or under a summer sun that refused to observe tradition and didn't set in time for dinner, looking at the evergreens, sniffing out wafts of jasmine, throwing rocks at cats in heat, or completely quiet.

Dinner at my parents' house was exhausting, with my mother organizing the table as if it were the foundation for a skyscraper, my father lost in thinking about some new legal tactic or a new addition to his stamp collection, or, worse, talking about these things. But it was more exhausting not to go, when the strange feeling we shared of being orphans with living parents overwhelmed us. So we went, and Rivkah could drink through the evening.

On the rare occasion that Simeon, in his way, convened his household for a dinner, or even a Saturday lunch, when Sara was again at home — now older, slow-moving, and unscattered — the event was entirely different from the ones that occurred at my parents' house. The old elegance returned, but now pared down, heavier, and more dignified because of it.

"Aaron, come in my boy," he said before one of those few dinners, calling me into his study. I could only see him as a sliver through the open crack in the door, standing in a deep light in the room as if etched into it, looking more like an obscure scholar than the magnate of business and power politics he in fact was. I creaked the door open, and realized, standing in my tailored clothes, wearing nice shoes, with all my experience as a man behind me, that Simeon was the one person I knew who could still make me feel like a boy.

I walked into the room and saw him peering over documents spread out on a desk, and him leaning heavily with a hand on the surface of the wood, supporting himself even though his body was still as strong, and even lean, as it had been years before.

He took off his glasses as he looked up and gave me his full attention. I looked around that enormous room, the library sunken in crimson hues with a catwalk above where another row of editions lined the walls. Below, here, was a simple space, just two chairs, the desk, a simple coffee table — no massive globe or any of the other library-room pretensions of the wealthy.

"Sit, please. It's wonderful to see you. Let me pour you a whiskey."

"Thank you, Gadi," I said, still having to make an effort to drop the "Mr." of my childhood and sputter out his first name. "How are you? You look good."

"I'm fine. Work is moving along, as it always does. Sara is off enjoying her travels, or, at least, doing what she feels she needs to do. But mostly, what makes me most happy, is to see my Rivkaleh in the world, and to see her with you."

I smiled, and nodded as if to thank him for the compliment.

"She is a rare thing, that one. But you know that. She loves you. You and Rivkah are the future, are my future, the future of our families."

I sipped the whiskey, and looked at his glass, which he didn't touch.

"Did I ever tell you how we gave her that name? Well, that's a little dishonest, since I know I never told anyone.

"I saw," he said, laughing at the memory, "the doctor's face when we informed him what the names on the birth certificates should be. I think his first reaction was to explain to me that the two names were the same, one the Anglicized, one the Hebraized version of the other.

"Obviously, he remembered himself, or remembered that I was not a complete idiot, and kept it to himself. Later, the nurse made some comment about it, which I forget, but Sara, holding them wriggling in her arms, looked at me and smiled at it.

"For years people wondered — who would do such a thing, what kind of arrogance was it to play a game with the names of our children? But I'd learned long before that, that in this world you need to act for yourself, to live your life the way it's important to you that it be lived. Tradition is something, convention is nothing. It's a simple equation, but a good one.

"I should tell you that I'm sorry for speaking like this — so heavy, and, it might seem, without considering you. How many speeches the young have had to endure from the old, it makes me a little ashamed to be adding another to that opus. But you're the only person in the world who, I feel, should hear this.

"Before our girls were born, before we had any of the tests done, we fantasized about who this child would be. We knew it was a girl. We knew some of the qualities she would have. She was to be the first real generation, all of us before just paving the road, fighting the wars, still standing with one foot in the desert.

"In the Torah it says that living in the Land, Yitzhak was told, *'Ein chutza la'Aretz kedai le'cha.'* It was time for them to stay, to be here, to be beyond return. We knew and felt our child should be this. Rivkah, the wife of Yitzhak. 'Rebecca,' as Sara's grandparents, living in America, would have once said.

"We should have known better: in the Torah, Rivkah herself had twins," he said, looking down with a smile. "So, Sara and I were not prophets of our children's future, though many parents think they are. But we wanted their birthright to be marked, and so we split the name, and they were Rivkah and Rebecca.

"I laughed then, when the doctors and nurses, and our cousins, uncles, nieces, and friends smirked or smiled at the names. Their reactions were always so set, so predictable. But, today, I can't laugh at it anymore. We thought there would be one of them, and now, even though it's still hard for me to believe, there is just one, just Rivkah, the other one gone.

"Aaron, my son, I sometimes thank God for you, that you're here, that you love Rivkah. For all of my power in the world, I wasn't able to keep this family from falling apart, or at least, changing irrevocably. But you have made something whole, you have kept something alive.

"You and Rivkah will inherit everything — more than the money, and the things, you will inherit the life we, the thousand generations, have struggled to build. It's yours, I'm not giving you anything, but just passing along what was given to me. What you choose to do with your life, with your days, is your business. Whatever it is, I am happy. Whatever Rivkah does, I am happy.

"I asked you here today not just to give you my blessing, which you have always had, but, in some strange way, to ask for yours. Maybe it's improper, but I want to ask you to bless our family with its future. I want to live, and die, with that knowledge. That way, I can still feel a sense of redemption. I can somehow feel that Rebecca's death — " he sobbed, then sighed, having spoken directly about his dead daughter for the first time in the conversation, maybe in years.

He was quiet for a few minutes. I sipped my drink, feeling the heat of sadness on my face, having released any notion of awkwardness of sitting with the great man without saying a thing. I had the feeling that both of us sat there half expecting a ten-year-old Rivkah to walk through that door to call us to dinner, or crying to us to tell us what wanton evil was done to her by her sister.

No one came. The room seemed to get darker. I finished my drink and was thinking we should go — leave the mess of tragedy again — when I realized that I hadn't answered him.

"I understand what you mean, Gadi. Whatever you need, I'll give it. You never needed me to promise to love Rivkah, but I'll make the promise anyways."

Simeon looked at me and smiled. He wanted to hug or kiss me, I could see, so I held out my hand. He shook it, and we got up to go to dinner.

It wasn't much later when that ancien régime was gone, and the rooms it once occupied, where it delivered its power and opened the blossom of its life sat unsold and empty. Rivkah and I had moved into our own home. After weeks of debating as we sat on European beaches during a badly needed vacation, we'd decided that we could not take the old house, as she always imagined we would. We found our own house, smaller, with fewer twists and turns, and none of the memories sleeping in the Simeon mansion.

But Rivkah insisted that we carry the tradition of the Great Shabbos. She was so invested in that belief that it was beyond consideration, and I knew that I could only accept it and play my part by trying to offer the speeches, the welcome, the intimate glow of dignity that had defined Simeon. I knew in this I would either find my own way or fail, but no matter what happened I could look to Rivkah and see her happiness as she spoke to the guests in Sara Simeon's marble tones, made sure the children at the table were appreciated, and executed a flawless menu and table in honor of the Bride of Shabbat.

In the weeks leading up to our first Shabbos dinner I watched as Rivkah prepared for the night with the coolness of an expert. There was never a hint of worry, or the notion that she might do something wrong. I came home from work the Wednesday before Shabbat and saw the table standing there like a newly built building, with structures and embellishments, the portico of plates and knives, the bas-relief of small vases, all existing in loving obedience to an architect.

I couldn't explain the nervousness I began to feel the moment I saw that table. It should have only been joy — with the birth of our son, and his health, with Rivkah's beauty refining itself every day, and the flush of motherhood on her cheeks, with our home's vaulted ceilings flying upward, leaving no shadows of vanity or vulgarity to mark it, with a sense that we were living as the fulfillment of the dreams of not just our parents but our heritage.

That evening moved closer toward us. I took my son out for a walk in the German Colony, to get Rivkah a single missing ingredient, an extra tablecloth, or a bunch of flowers, and walked in the late afternoon sunshine still impressed by my wife's beauty. But the evening still came closer, still approached, and when it arrived I found myself agitated as I passed in front of the open bathroom door where Rivkah sat in front of her mirror, quietly and simply dressing and putting on her makeup, touching each eyelash, smoothing every hair.

That evening, I struggled to put on the cufflinks that my father had left me in his will. He had, of course, also left me his fortune, his home, the books, a sheath of copyrights, but these were all included in the "everything" that was left to his only son. Only the cufflinks, one or two antiquarian books, and his tallit were left by name and mention.

It was another little practical joke of my father's, I thought, giving me almost-broken cufflinks that I would have to struggle to put on, but also couldn't refuse. I dropped one, and saw its glint as it hit the carpet, and saw my father's haughty wink as the light flashed across his initials, and thought about the day and the moment he died, when he apologized to me in two words that were more simple than anything he'd ever said to me.

"I'm sorry," he said, and I listened, and thought and decided that I could forgive him my childhood, his distance, his isolating laughter. I thought I should tell him that I forgave him, so he could travel through death without the added burden of an unresolved apology. I said what I had to say and he opened his eyes and smiled — not a smile of redemption, but of irony.

As I struggled to close the cufflink, Rivkah sat serenely, even philosophically, in front of her mirror. I managed to get the first one closed, and then looked up to find where I'd the put the other one. Nervously, I looked at my wife to see if she was almost ready, but I didn't see Rivkah. I looked and didn't see my wife and the mother of my child, but saw the face of the woman sitting opposite to her — a face of equal age and verbatim beauty — and watched as the other woman looked at me, taking the diamond necklace off and in its place lifting a gold chain attached to a small gem that her mother had once given her as a child.

She lifted her elbows to clasp the chain behind her neck and I understood for the first time that my father never had, never could have, apologized for himself. What I took for an apology, I realized, was a final gesture of protection over his child, a condolence for what he saw was my tragedy.

I stood there on the evening of the Great Shabbos staring at the woman in the mirror whom I had always and will always love, and felt the spread of shame as I realized she had always been with me — that my love for Rivkah was a counterfeit love. And finally, as I closed the clasp of the second cufflink, I looked at Rebecca sitting silently in the mirror, smiling at me with her mute love, and in a moment of self-damnation and ultimate betrayal, I told her that I loved her.

❦❦❦

CPSIA information can be obtained
at www.ICGtesting.com
Printed in the USA
BVHW081221261221
624761BV00006BA/376